Likely Story:

All That Glitters

Likely Story: All That Glitters

David Van Etten

Alfred A. Knopf

New York

THIS IS A BORZOI BOOK PUBLISHED BY ALFRED A. KNOPF

Visit us on the Web! www.randomhouse.com/teens

Educators and librarians, for a variety of teaching tools, visit us at
www.randomhouse.com/teachers

Library of Congress Cataloging-in-Publication Data
Van Etten, David.
Likely story : all that glitters / David Van Etten. — 1st ed.
        p. cm.
Summary: Now that her soap opera is in production and everyone has ideas on how it can be improved, sixteen-year-old Mallory struggles to maintain control of her original plot and characters as the broadcast premiere draws near.
ISBN 978-0-375-84678-6 (trade) — ISBN 978-0-375-94678-3 (lib. bdg.)
[1. Television—Production and direction—Fiction. 2. Soap operas—Fiction.
3. Interpersonal relations—Fiction. 4. Self-confidence—Fiction. 5. Mothers and daughters—Fiction. 6. Hollywood (Los Angeles, Calif.)—Fiction.] I. Title. II. Title: All that glitters.
PZ7.V2746Lik 2008
[Fic]—dc22
2007050903

The text of this book is set in 13-point Galena.

Printed in the United States of America
October 2008
10 9 8 7 6 5 4 3 2 1

First Edition

Random House Children's Books supports the First Amendment
and celebrates the right to read.

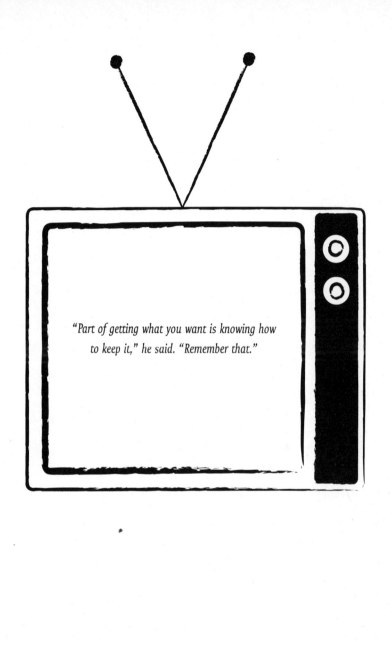

"Part of getting what you want is knowing how to keep it," he said. "Remember that."

o n e

I have a confession to make: My life is not nearly as glamorous as it might seem. Or as easy.

If I say, "I'm a sixteen-year-old girl who gets to run her own soap opera on network TV," it should mean big parties, great shoes, famous friends, and cash coming out of fountains.

The reality? TV seems a whole lot different when you're up at the crack of dawn making it. Famous doesn't look so sexy at 6 a.m.

Do you know what the world record for thinking *I have no idea what I'm doing* is? I think it's two million times in a single day. Which was pretty much a typical day for me as my show, *Likely Story,* came to life.

My skin tone had turned mortician-ready from all the time I spent untanning under fluorescent lights. Southern California living usually allows for plenty of sun; it gives the city populace its opulent glow. But the only color I had came from the sequoia-worthy rings under my eyes. I should have been able to deal with it. After all, I'd grown up on a soap opera set, the daughter of a Daytime Star. But it's one thing to be the little girl making lipstick drawings on the makeup table while her mother is twenty feet away, bitch-slapping a nun for stealing her husband. It's quite another thing to be the one responsible for every bitch slap, betrayal, and love quadrangle.

I needed a break from all the drama.

Finally I finagled a night off, despite my executive producer Richard's objections that there was still work to be done. One thing I'd learned quickly was that there was *always* work to be done, and if I wanted time off, I had to demand it. Or I had to sneak away.

There was no question about who I'd spend my freedom with. For reasons that weren't entirely clear, my ridiculously understanding boyfriend, Keith, had stuck with me even though I now spent much more time alone in my room writing about kissing than I did . . . well . . . kissing. So a big date was long overdue. While most guys would have used this as an opportunity to make a reservation at the closest cozy couch, Keith was taking me out for a special night at the movies. One of my favorite classics—*Cat on a Hot Tin Roof,* starring Liz Taylor and Paul Newman as a Southern couple whose marriage is slowly eaten away by the secret that they harbor. (One of them is in love with another man. Guess which.) My mother had gotten me hooked on the movie years ago, while she was researching her role as Liz Taylor in the Lifetime Original Movie *A Diamond Cuts Both Ways: The Nine Lives and Seven Loves of Elizabeth Taylor.* It was not a memorable MOW (that's Movie of the Week in biz speak) and did not serve as the launching pad to the greater cable success my mother had been hoping for. It had, however, instilled in me an early love for the weepy but wonderful women drawn by that maestro of melodrama, Ten-

4

nessee Williams. I had been looking forward to the movie all week. There was only one problem: As much as I loved Tennessee Williams and Liz Taylor and Keith and the idea of going out on a date, I loved sleep even more. And as much as I'd been neglecting Keith, I'd been neglecting sleep even more.

My eyes started to close as soon as the opening credits began to roll.

The next thing I knew, Keith was whispering, "Mallory. Mallory! Wake up!"

"Huh?" I asked groggily, taking in his rough-boy-makes-nice features. "Is something on fire?"

"Erika is here."

I bolted awake. Erika was his ex-girlfriend—the one he'd been dating when he'd started seeing me. When he'd finally broken up with her, she'd threatened to kill herself, kill him, and kill me. Not necessarily in that order.

So—not a fire, but definitely a five-alarm emergency.

"She's here?!" I asked, just to make certain.

"Uh-huh. Two rows in front of us, four seats over."

"Why couldn't the cat have stayed on the damn tin roof?"

Keith gave me a withering glance and I knew I shouldn't have said that. I absolutely respected the fact that he still cared about Erika's well-being. I just didn't particularly want to see it.

"Do you mind if we sneak out before she sees us?" he asked. "You know how fragile she is. I don't want her to see us together."

"But I love this movie," I said. What I meant was, *I thought the fact that you broke up with her and started dating me full-time meant we didn't have to sneak around anymore.*

"You were out cold."

Keith's eyes were pleading now. I couldn't say no to that.

"Let's go, Brick," I said.

"Thanks, Maggie. I owe you one."

We exited the theater as lo-pro as possible. At the back of the theater I stopped for just a moment to enjoy my favorite line from the whole movie. Liz Taylor, dressed only in a white slip (*très* scandalous in the fifties), is clawing the back of the settee, screeching at her husband, Brick, "Skipper is dead! I'm alive! Maggie the Cat is ALIVE!" That's the right attitude, Liz. Fight for what you want.

"Sorry about falling asleep on you," I said when we got outside.

"That's cool. I know you're totally exhausted."

Totally exhausted didn't even begin to cover it. I was getting three, maybe four hours of sleep every night, juggling scripts and set questions and casting issues and meeting after meeting with the networks, the staff, the stars, and the sponsors. Oh, and I had to do schoolwork, too. It felt like the only time I had to think was when I was alone in an elevator.

"I didn't realize how much it was going to kill me," I admitted. "Once we get on the air, it will mellow out . . . I think."

"You think?" Keith asked doubtfully.

"A girl can dream, can't she?"

Keith smiled and pulled me close to him. "How 'bout a trip to Canter's to make up for the ex-girlfriend drama? I think some latkes and applesauce is just what you need."

This is why we go through all the confusion and pain and compromise to be in a couple, isn't it? Just to have someone say, *This is what you need,* and to have it be true. If he'd asked me what I needed at that moment, I never would have been able to say it. I would have just stared at him blankly, not knowing. But instead, he gave it to me. He knew, even if I didn't.

I kissed him quickly. Not just for knowing me, but for wanting to.

Canter's Delicatessen is one of the few real "haunts" in Los Angeles, a city that eats its history faster than models can hide their dinner in napkins. Open twenty-four hours, it caters to the eclectic Hollywood clientele that needs corned beef sandwiches and pickles at all hours of the day. Now, by "Hollywood," I don't mean the movie star variety but rather old men who used to "work in pictures" and scruffy, tipsy screenwriters wooing bronzed bimbos with tri-color hair.

As a surly woman named Deena led me and Keith to our table, I marveled at the plastic Tiffany-style ceiling and the way it cast a queer orange and yellow glow, making everyone inside look like they had liver disease. That was always one of the reasons I never ordered the liver and onions. (The other reason being that liver and onions is disgusting.) Keith ordered the Monte Cristo with extra syrup and I had the latkes (potato pancakes to goyim like me) with extra applesauce.

I was just starting to relax when Keith asked, "So what are you gonna do about the opening credits?"

I shrugged. I didn't really want to talk about work. Because lately it seemed that's all I ever did. It was nice that Keith cared enough to ask. So many other guys would have been competitive about it. Or would have been liking me for my job, not for who I was. But I knew Keith still saw me as a normal girl with totally abnormal responsibilities. Or at least that's how I hoped he saw me.

"We're still figuring the opening credits out," I told him. Which was the polite version of: *I am in so over my head that I can't even figure out how the show starts.*

Our waitress dropped off my coffee and Keith's milk shake. As I took my first sip, I noticed a familiar-looking duo across the restaurant: my former-best-friend Amelia and her kissing-bandit brother, Jake.

I reached across the table and grabbed Keith's hand. "Don't turn around," I warned.

"Famous person?" Keith asked in a hushed tone.

"No. It's Amelia and her brother." I sank lower into my seat, trying to hide behind the creamer and pickles. First Erika, now this. All I needed was the third-grade teacher who told our class that Mallory was a boy's name, and my humiliation would be complete.

"Can we go somewhere else?" I pleaded.

It was one thing to face off with Erika—even if she wanted to tear me apart, I didn't really think she would touch me. But Amelia, on the other hand, could rip me to shreds with a single glance. It had been a while since we'd last talked, a while since I'd told her she couldn't be the lead in *Likely Story*. I'd told her the truth—that she wasn't good enough—and she'd called me names that most newspapers wouldn't publish. When it came to destroying our friendship, I hadn't just pulled the pin on the grenade—I'd sat on it. Now it hurt every time I had something I wanted to tell her. One by one, our happy memories turned sour. She hated me now more than she'd ever liked me as a best friend.

"You know, Mal, you didn't do anything wrong," Keith tried to console. "If she really wants to be an actress, she's gonna have to get used to rejection."

"But being rejected by your best friend is a different story."

"She's been acting like a complete witch," he said. "Everybody knows that."

"Then why does everyone at school refuse to talk to me? Or if they do, it's to call me a celebutard?"

"They're just jealous. You get to leave school early almost every day—if you even come at all—and when you're there, you're too busy texting Richard to notice them. That's why they play along when she says you're all high-and-mighty."

"Do you think I am?" I wondered sheepishly.

"Of course not. And even celebutards have a right to eat Jewish food in peace. We're not going anywhere."

This was sort of twisted, since he'd just made me leave my favorite movie to avoid his messy past, but I supposed he was right.

"It makes me sad to not have a best friend anymore," I confided.

Keith came around to my side of the booth and put his arm around me.

"You have me," he offered.

"Thanks. I know." Not entirely the same thing, but still sweet.

Keith started to comfort me some more, but we were interrupted.

"Hi, Mallory." It was Jake. His grin was its usual happy-evil.

I feigned surprise. "Oh, Jake, what are you doing here?"

"My sister wanted me to give you this." He dropped a folded paper napkin on the table. "See ya around. I can give you a ride sometime."

I felt myself blushing. The last time I'd been in his front seat, I'd come dangerously close to treating it like a backseat. A momentary lapse of sanity.

"Maybe it's a peace offering," Keith said, pointing to the napkin. "Read it." I opened it and tried to keep a poker face. In pink ink, from what I knew to be Amelia's favorite pink pen, the napkin read:

> YOU ARE A SKANKY BACKSTABBING
> SKANK.
> XOXO AMELIA

My poker face fell. I'd been dealt a really bad hand.

"Let's get our food to go," Keith said. "Waitress!"

I couldn't help looking over at Amelia, who stuck out her tongue and raised a middle finger.

I wished there was a gesture I could send back her way—maybe a raised pinkie to mean "I'm sorry." Or an index finger–pinkie combo to mean "Give me another chance." You see, that was the thing that hurt the most—not that she was angry, but that I secretly thought she had every right to be angry. She felt I'd chosen my show over our friendship. I hadn't meant to. I never would have meant to.

But maybe I had.

Maybe I was the type of person who would stop at nothing to be successful.

And odds were good that I'd end up a failure anyway.

"That's what happens when you get successful—you
find enemies lurking around every corner. . . ."

t w o

Back in the car, after our takeout meal was finished, Keith tried to kiss me into a better mood. But then I had to leave the car and head back to reality again.

Unfortunately, that reality contained my mother.

I know that some girls can go to their moms and have heart-to-heart talks. With my mom, it was more like heart-to-fangs.

After a long and rather pleasant goodbye with Keith (heart-to-mouth-to-mouth-to-heart), I forced myself up the garden path, past the gazebo and swan pond, hoping to delay my confrontation with Mom for as long as possible. Through the kitchen bay window, on the other side of the never-used copper pots and pans that hung above the center island, I saw her. She was working through the better part of a bottle of Grey Goose vodka. To make matters worse, she was mixing it with the nasty pomegranate juice her trainer had convinced her was "cleansing." I didn't think it was going to do much cleansing when it was cut with alcohol.

I came in through the back door.

"Welcome home, sweetie," she said with a beam. Immediately I knew something was up. When my mother tries to imitate a nice person, there's usually a big hitch underneath.

"How was your evening out with the beauhunk?" she slurred, her teeth stained purple by the juice.

"If you really want to know, we ran into his ex-girlfriend at the movie and then were ambushed by Amelia at Canter's."

"That's what happens when you get successful—you find enemies lurking around every corner. That's why God invented VIP rooms."

Mom was always worried that her VIP status would go RIP. She'd come pretty close lately when her show, *Good As Gold*, was dropped by the network. But like the woman on the *Titanic* who just happened to have a lifeboat in her pocketbook, my mother managed to survive that one . . . by being given a part on my show. It was her most effective maternal ambush to date.

I hadn't really had a say about whether to hire my mom for *Likely Story* . . . but I *did* have a say in what character she'd play. Things had been pretty tense around the old homestead as we haggled over what her role would be. Since she somehow managed to wrangle "character approval" from the network in her new contract, I was forced to shoehorn her into my show in a way she found appealing. My first ideas had been met with scowls—or at least what her Botoxed face could approximate as a scowl. When I suggested a humpback librarian, she literally spit on the script and said she'd sooner play Benjamin Franklin than play deformed. I spent three days after that trying to work the ghost of Benjamin Franklin into the show. It didn't work. Even worse than her rejecting my ideas was when she tried to come up with ideas of her own. "What if I play a high-powered newspaper editor with a penchant for younger men?" she'd suggested. I pointed out that this was the same exact character (give or take a few personalities) she had played on *Good As Gold*. She scoffed at my ignorance and retorted that she had played a *magazine* editor, not a *newspaper* editor—they were two *totally* different things.

Eventually, after a few more volleys that included such classics as the Ghost of Deception Past (my idea) and Melinda the psychic pharmaceutical heiress (her idea), we settled on the notion that she would be the guidance counselor at Deception Pass High School. Since my mother's idea of "guidance" is "Which way to the bar?" and her idea of "counseling" is "That scarf makes your whole body look fat," we took certain liberties with the character's past. In other words, she wasn't just a guidance counselor but *an aging movie star in witness protection who was masquerading as a guidance counselor*. Of course I didn't use the word "aging" when I pitched the idea to her. I said "former." So now that she didn't have to be worried that I'd make her a great-grandmother or a Founding Father on the show, there wasn't any real reason for her to pretend to be nice to me. But her Kindergarten Teacher Voice was back as she sweetly asked, "Are you ready for your big day tomorrow?"

"It's a Monday—are those really bigger than the other days of the week?" I responded as I poured myself a glass of orange juice.

"It's not just any Monday—it's *cast photo Monday*," she reminded me, making another Pomtini. "We're taking a portrait for the cover of *Soap Opera Bi-Weekly*."

"What do you mean, *we*?" I asked. The last time I'd checked, I wasn't a member of the cast.

"Hasn't Richard told you?" My mother halfheartedly attempted to put some surprise in her voice. "I'm positively sure it was in that memo. You, me, and Dallas are going to be on the cover. Isn't it a scream?"

If by *scream* she meant Edvard Munch's panicked painting, then yes, I was about to slap my hands on my cheeks and howl. "Me? I'm not a cover girl! I never agreed to this."

"I'm sure your contract says you are willing and able to participate in any and all publicity for the show."

"It does not!" I argued, though I had a feeling she was right. All those little paragraphs and sub-paragraphs that were part of a legally binding contract had a way of sneaking up on a girl.

And that wasn't the only thing sneaking up on me. There was also my mom's mention of Dallas, the star of my show. Every time I saw him, I got that little shiver of excitement. And hearing his name was like an echo of that shiver. Not just because he was beautiful. But because my show's future was resting on his shoulders. And it felt right for it to be there.

A whole photo shoot, with us posing so close to each other. After I had spent months making sure I didn't have any reason whatsoever to touch him.

I didn't want to think about it. And I didn't want my mother to think about me thinking about it.

"Want some Pom?" she asked.

"No, Mom. No Pom," I said as I gulped down the last of my OJ. "I'm going to my room."

As I walked up the stairs, I heard her call after me, "Are we still carpooling to work tomorrow?"

I didn't answer her. I swear, she was *enjoying* this.

I got to my room and looked at the pile of half-written scripts littering the floor. My computer blinked at me. Only 157 new e-mails. Probably all of them urgent. I was hopelessly behind on my life. So I dealt with it the only way I knew how: by dropping onto the bed and falling asleep before I could even take my Steve Madden boots off.

So this is what I dreamed. I would spend the next day trying to block it out of my mind.

The hot Mexican air wafted through the beachside cabana while I sipped a virgin daiquiri. I grabbed some sunscreen from a table littered with the leftovers of our lobster quesadillas and bent down to kiss my napping Keith on the forehead. He looked so cute, passed out like a bum in the sun. His trunks were riding up his thighs, caught on the chaise lounge. His hair was pasted to his forehead, still wet from his pre-brunch dip in the warm Gulf waters. *I am such a lucky girl,* I thought to myself.

Walking out from the shady cabana to the beach itself, I couldn't believe this was really happening. Where had Keith gotten the money to whisk me off to Puerto Vallarta? I didn't know and, frankly, I didn't care to ask. It would take a lot of extra hours at California Pizza Kitchen to afford a flight down here.

The sand was burning my feet, so I quickly darted the few feet to where my towel and magazines lay. Rubbing my arms with lotion, I stared out into the Gulf of Mexico and smiled to myself. It was so great to be away from all the stress of *Likely Story*. I reclined back on my hotel towel and grabbed the copy of *Night of the Iguana* I'd picked up at Sam French before heading on the trip. Just as I cracked the spine, Keith came up behind me.

"Hey, Tennessee," Keith said.

"Hey, Minnesota," I replied. "How was your nap?"

"Four stars." Keith sat down next to me on the towel and cooed in my ear, "I want to go parasailing."

"Have fun. I'll wave to you from here."

"Come on, Mallory, I want you to go, too."

"If I para-sail, I will end up para-plegic."

Keith shook his head and stood up. "You're hopeless." He started doing yoga poses, salutating the sun and whatnot. This was strange, since I'd never seen him do yoga before. I returned to the play but couldn't get a focus on it. It seemed as if all the words were swimming around the page like sea monkeys. I looked up to the horizon, blinking my eyes. It was then that I noticed the slow darkening of the sky. The light was sepia-toned, making everything look like an old photograph. I figured I was getting too much sun. How long had we been here in Mexico? Didn't I have work to do in the States? Were all those scripts really finished?

It was then that things started getting really weird. Was I crazy, or did I recognize that shimmering young man emerging from the salty waters? The rivulets of water streaming down his chest glistened like semiprecious stones. Yes, I did recognize him. What was Dallas doing here?

"Mallory!" he called out. "I've been looking everywhere for you. I have something important to tell you."

I glanced over at Keith, who was oddly oblivious to all this as he continued to do ever-more-complicated yoga poses. Wow. Keith was good. But I returned my gaze to Dallas. I held my hand up above my eyes to shield them from the sun. The eerie sun made Dallas's hair shine. My heart was beating fast.

"What are you doing in Mexico?" I asked.

"I came for you, Mallory. I love you."

As if in a trance, I rose up. Dallas took my face in his hands and drew it close.

Beep beep beep beep beep

It was like my conscience had an alarm. Only in this case, it was really my clock that had the alarm.

Normally, I don't waste much time on dream analysis. But I didn't need Sigmund Freud to tell me this one meant something.

It was almost beautiful, how he trusted me.
Now I'd just have to deserve it.

three

Six a.m. had arrived much too soon. I was discovering a hard truth: There's no way to catch up on sleep. When it's gone, it's gone, and the best you can hope for is to have better luck next time.

I groggily stumbled to the kitchen in my pajamas and poured a massive cup of coffee. My mother was already up and dressed.

"The car will be here in about twenty-five minutes, so you'd better shower and get dressed pronto," she said without looking up from the *LA Times* Calendar section. "You should wear that new outfit I got you from Marc Jacobs—you know, the jacket and skirt with the black velvet trim."

"I don't know, Mom—it's not really my style."

"That's your first problem—you have no style. If you want to keep the crew's respect, you have to look like you deserve it. Marc Jacobs says, 'I enjoy simplicity but I still have exquisite taste.'"

I stared at my mother blankly. I needed more coffee.

Twenty-three minutes later I was in the Marc Jacobs suit with my hair pulled up into a twist. It looked better than I expected—like I was playing a game of Celebrity Court Date with my friends.

The black sedan honked from outside the gate. My mother was waiting by the door, and I followed her out into the bright and crisp morning sun, her heels clacking on the cobblestone driveway. The Mercedes gleamed, and I must admit it was a step up from the school bus.

I scooted into the backseat with my bag full of scripts, notebooks, and a travel cup of coffee. Did I bring my laptop? Yes. Check.

As we drove down the winding streets of the hills above LA, I looked through my to-do list:

1. Production Meeting
2. Writers' Meeting
3. Meeting with Richard
4. Photo Shoot
5. Come Up with a New Week of Storylines
6. Pull My Hair Out
7. Buy Valentine's Day Present for Keith

The third thing on my list became number one with a silver bullet when I saw Richard waiting at the parking spot when we pulled in.

"Mallory! You're late," he chastised as soon as I got within chastising range.

He was in his usual black designer shirt and slacks, capped by shiny leather loafers on one end and small, razor-thin sunglasses on the other. His slicked-and-gelled hair glistened like a shellacked bathing cap.

"Traffic," I explained. It's the go-to excuse for everything in LA.

"Morning, darling," my mother called to him as she was helped out of the car by the driver.

"Beautiful day, isn't it?" he responded with a smile.

"It's why we live here," she said back as she sauntered away toward makeup, leaving me to stand in front of the anger train.

I looked at my watch. "The meeting with the network is in ten minutes. I'm not late."

"Maybe if you had been here at sunrise, we would have been able to discuss things."

"Discuss what?" I said cautiously.

"It's too late. You'll just have to find out in real time."

Real time. Right. The set of a TV show is like high school . . . but worse because everyone is getting paid a lot of money to be there. That much money at stake makes everyone nervous, so the backstabbing is done with machetes, not butter knives; the double-crossing becomes quadruple-crossing; and the rumors fly like foam from a rabid dog's mouth.

"Fine," I said in huff. Richard was always pulling this passive-aggressive act. Like he was totally trying to do me a favor but my ineptitude prevented his every effort. I wanted to tell him to stop treating me like his spoiled niece—but I knew that would only make me sound like I was his spoiled niece. The key to working with Richard was proving that I could be just as professional as he was. Whatever that meant.

"I'm going to grab a danish from craft services, since there's no way I'm facing the network on an empty stomach," I told him. "Then I'll see you upstairs."

"Avoid the apple this morning," Richard told me. "The cherry isn't nearly as stale."

This was perhaps the most frustrating thing about Richard—after giving me grief, he'd dollop out a small dose of friendly help, leaving me completely confounded.

I walked over to craft services and found all four of my lead actors shuffling around, in costume but not yet needed on the set. I walked over to the table and took my place next to Javier Sabato, who played Marco, our bad boy with a heart of gold. He was wearing tattered jeans that clearly were hand-distressed in some third-world sweatshop, a perfectly vintage Bob Dylan *Blonde on Blonde* T-shirt, and cowboy boots. The red-wine scent of his dark brooding wafted over to me from across the juice selection.

"Wow—the costume department did a great job. You look like such a tragic hipster," I said.

Javier looked up from his breakfast of danish and Fritos and leveled a glance my way. "Don't even get me started, girl. Those witches of wardrobe don't know Marco like I do. I spent hours searching through racks at Crossroads to get these clothes. The one on Ventura, *not* the one in West Hollywood—even though the WeHo one has some better stuff sometimes 'cause it's less picked over. You know, WeHo boys hate used things."

I felt Javier was much better suited to say what West Hollywood boys loved or hated than I was, so I just nodded. Luckily, Marco's tale of wardrobe dysfunction was interrupted by Alexis, who played the female lead, Sarah, on the show.

"Be careful of the apple danish this morning," she warned. Unlike the rest of us, she seemed fully awake—even though, freakishly, she never drank any caffeine. It was awkward for me at first with Alexis, because she had the part I'd written for Amelia. But I had to admit: Alexis was a super-good actress. She also had a really pushy stage mom (who Richard had barred from the set). It seemed like Alexis's way of rebelling was not to rebel—so far, she'd been the kind of actress who bakes cookies for the crew . . . and doesn't stay around for compliments about them. If anything, I found her a little boring. But with so many other large personalities around, I was grateful for a little boredom.

"I love your outfit," she said to me now. "Aren't you excited for photo day?"

"I'll put the 'polar' in Polaroid," I mumbled.

Alexis giggled. "You're so funny," she said, taking a nectarine and heading to her dressing room.

Javier had run off the moment the center of attention had shifted away from him, so I made my way to the other two stars of the show, Francesca and Dallas. They had been together at Juilliard before coming out to California for *Likely Story,* and I was never really certain what their particular togetherness involved. I wanted to think they were benefitless friends, but every now and then they'd lean into each other or hold hands and I'd feel like Nancy Drew on the Case of the Completely Confusing Couple. This was why I wanted all couples to wear rings, not just married ones. Different colors for different stages—baby blue for *we're just starting out,* yellow for *cautiously figuring it out,* red for *making out but not making future plans,* green for *happy together,* and then the usual gold and/or silver for *voluntarily shackled to each other for eternity.* It would just make life easier.

Their heads were practically touching over the table as they talked, the crumbs of their breakfast the only things within hearing range. When they saw me coming, they pulled back a little and stopped talking. Francesca shot Dallas a glance. Dallas shot a glance back at her.

When I finally got over to them, Francesca stood up. She was naturally thin, naturally tall, and not naturally friendly— we were never going to be sleepover sisters. It was going to be work just to get her to thaw to basic human kindness.

"The camera calls," she said with a sigh.

"Good morning!" I called out a second too late.

I didn't want to sit down at the table if Dallas was going to leave, so instead I teetered awkwardly until he said, "Join me for a sec."

Dallas played Ryan, the hero of *Likely Story.* Both were handsome, decent, conflicted—in other words, that undeniably flawed guy that every girl wants. The weird thing was, I'd created Ryan before I even knew Dallas existed. Then Dallas showed up and it was like I'd been writing him all along.

This was one of many reasons I felt awkward around him. Right now was a special kind of awkward, the kind reserved for when you have an intense dream about someone and then you see him the next morning. You know it's completely impossible for him to know that you dreamed about him . . . and at the same time, the dream was so intense that you feel he *must* know.

He was staring at me, and for a second I truly thought he was going to say, "Mexico? Why Mexico?"

But instead he said, "New look for you?"

Damn you, Marc Jacobs. Damn you!

"I like it," he added.

Thank you, Marc Jacobs. Thank you!

"It's my disguise," I explained. "For when I have to play a grown-up."

"We've all heard about the network meeting," he said as I dug into my coffee cake.

"Yeah, well . . . ," I said between bites. I didn't want him to know I was completely clueless about the meeting. I wanted him to think I was on top of everything.

"Just don't give in, okay?" His gaze was so strong on me that I had to look down at my paper plate.

"Is that what you and Francesca were talking about?" I dared to ask.

"That, and other things. She thinks we'll all be forced to compromise. But I told her you wouldn't. She said I was too optimistic. I told her that wasn't always a bad thing."

"Don't worry," I assured him. "The whole reason I got this show was because I wanted to do something different. Something meaningful. They can't change that."

He smiled, relieved. "I feel better already," he said. "And I promise, it isn't just the clothes you're wearing."

It was almost beautiful, how he trusted me.

Now I'd just have to deserve it.

I made my way toward the bungalows that housed the network honchos' offices. They were at the center of the studio lot, nestled around a tranquil green that masked the "creative minds" working their TV magic in cauldrons hidden discreetly behind French doors and latticework.

Richard met me in the hallway.

"Trip's meeting with the execs in New York," he told me. "So this is Webster's meeting."

I tried not to groan. Trip Carver was the Daytime president at the network . . . and also my mother's latest ex-husband. He was about as fake as a plastic flamingo, but at least I knew how to deal with him. Webster Strong, the Vice President of Daytime Strategy, was much worse. He made the grim reaper seem like a character from *Sesame Street*. I always dreaded meetings with him, not only because he was old and hideous, but because his office smelled vaguely of the antiseptic in an ICU. Probably because of all the promising careers of writers, actors, and general-purpose dreamers that had flatlined after failing him. His big nighttime show had been *Borderline,* about an all-female squad of Border Patrol agents who hunted illegal aliens as dangerous as the squad members were sexy. It had lasted four mind-numbingly bad episodes, and he'd been switched to daytime soon thereafter.

"You ready?" Richard asked me, his hand on the doorknob.

Just once in my life, I'd like to be able to answer that question with a "yes" I really meant.

But this was not going to be that time.

"*You were raised by soaps. You know how it works.
Beat 'em at their own game.*"

f o u r

We walked into the conference room. Webster Strong sat at the head of the table, the morning sun shining and bouncing off his bald head.

"There's our little wunderkind!" he shouted. "How's my favorite genius?"

I smiled nervously. Around the room was a motley crew of high-powered execs who did such exciting things as branding! marketing! advertising! and sales! I sat between the young woman who had some title like Director of Television Futures and another, grayer woman who I knew to be Vice President of Brand Management. I didn't know what either of them actually did besides get paid and wear expensive Italian shoes.

As was my habit in network meetings, I looked immediately to my one unquestionable ally: Trip Carver's assistant, Greg. Luckily, he was still in the room, taking notes, even though Trip was off on the other coast. As usual, he looked like he was playing dress-up in his suit and tie. We were the sneaker kids stuck in a loafer-and-heels world. Normally, Greg would send me a big smile over the table. This time, though, he looked worried. Which made me worried.

Webster continued, "We've all had a chance to watch a handful of your shows, and let me be the first to tell you how excited we are." The minions all nodded in agreement. "We absolutely love it," he continued. Again the minions nodded. "Trip wanted me to tell you that, too."

"I can't tell you what a relief that is," I said. "We're really proud of the work we've been doing, aren't we, Richard?"

I met Richard's eyes, but he didn't automatically respond. "Aren't we, Richard?" I repeated.

"Yes, we're very proud," Richard finally said.

"It's because this project is so great that we wanted to give you just a few notes on how we could make it even better," Webster said.

I gulped. I'd already been through enough with the network to know that "just a few notes" never meant "just a few notes." It's like when the dentist says, "This will only hurt for a second," and you end up sore for days.

Webster turned to the very blond woman at his left. "Holly, why don't you handle this?" he commanded.

Immediately Holly Hughes, VP of Daytime Development, sat up at attention and began shuffling through some papers in front of her. "Let me just reiterate how much we *love* this project. But we were wondering if there might be a way to spice things up."

"Oka-a-ay," I said, feeling like I was walking into a trap. "How spicy are you thinking? Mild? Medium? Hot? Fire Sauce?"

"I couldn't help but notice," Holly went on, "that even after five episodes, none of the characters are having sex. Why aren't they having sex?"

"That's not what this show is about," I explained. "The characters will have sex when it would make sense for them to have sex—that's not where they are in their relationships right now."

"My niece lost her virginity at fourteen," one of the execs chimed in.

"Fourteen?" another threw in. "My son was *twelve*."

"Problems and danger are the currency of this genre, Mallory," Holly said condescendingly. "Soaps are about romance—and nothing causes more problems in romance than sex. I just think that even if *you* are afraid of sex, your *characters* shouldn't be."

"I am *not* afraid of *sex*," I said. "Although I *am* afraid of middle-aged women who love the idea of teenagers doing it."

It was at this point that Greg knocked over his water glass and Richard started choking on what could have only been the remnants of the morning's apple danish.

I gathered my thoughts. Even though I'd scored a point against her, it was also two points against me for rising to the bait and throwing her comment back in her face like a resentful teenager. I took a long breath and said, "If we start them out at level ten, there's nowhere to go. I mean, shouldn't we *work* up to them having sex? We have a lot of stories to tell—it seems foolish to work too fast."

"Point taken," Webster said, leaning back in his chair and rubbing the bridge of his nose. "But that doesn't solve the problem."

"I don't understand," I said. "What's the problem?"

Holly barked, "The show is BORING, Mallory. No one cares about watching people do algebra homework. They want excitement, sizzle—all the things that are lacking in their own lives. They won't tune in to watch people doing things just like them."

"But this show is supposed to be *real*. It's supposed to be like life. And I don't have people doing *algebra homework*."

"There's a fine line between real and dull," Webster said in his dead monotone. "Like the reality shows on MTV are real, but they're still sexy."

"There's nothing real about those shows on MTV! Who has a Jacuzzi in the middle of their kitchen?" I asked rhetorically. However, my point was lost because four hands around the table shot up. Oy.

Frieda Weiner (pronounced "whiner"), one of the network's "consultants," spoke up. "We're just spitballing ideas here," she cawed. "For instance, I was thinking that maybe one of the boys could get involved with your mom's character. You know, one of those sexy student-teacher relationships. Don't tell me that's not real. I've seen *Dateline*."

I felt like someone had dipped me in honey and thrown me into a pit of bees and bears. I was not about to write scenes where my *mother* had sex with Dallas. Or kissed him. Or even passed him a note. Not a chance.

"These are just suggestions," Webster said calmly, but I could see he was starting to itch from his own gangrene.

Stay calm, I reminded myself. *Stay calm*.

"I just think that you could give us a chance to be real before you start throwing in the affairs," I said. "Next you'll want alien babies and amnesia."

"It's a little early for amnesia, but I do like the alien baby idea. It's been years since we've seen that on a soap," Frieda Weiner offered.

"See—it's been done. Help me out here, Richard," I pleaded. But he remained silent, so I was forced to fight the bees and the bears myself. "I thought the whole point of this was to do something new.. Something the viewers haven't seen."

"Blah, blah, blah, originality," Holly said dismissively. "We are in the business of selling what people want. And what people want is what they expect. On soaps, this means sex, scandal, and suspicion. No one cares if Marco finishes his book report on time. We have canceled one of the longest-running and most successful soap operas in history in order to give yours a shot. Don't make us regret dropping *Good As Gold*. We'll throw on repeats of test patterns if they get higher ratings than *Likely Story*."

"You're threatening to cancel the show? We haven't even aired yet!" I slammed my hands down on the table in exasperation.

Across from me, Richard was finally getting worried. "I think we're getting off on the wrong foot," he said. "Obviously Mallory is very passionate about this show. As am I. As are you." He gestured to all the idiots around us. "With all this passion, I'm sure we can find something we all agree on."

Webster breathed in deep. Everyone waited to hear what he would say next. After an exaggerated silence, he finally spoke. "Let me be frank—we don't like the first episodes and we don't think the audience will, either. Ryan's initial storyline has him working hard to save up money in order to take

Jacqueline on a fancy date, even though the person he really wants to take on the date is Sarah. That's nice, but I want murder. Blackmail. Abduction. I don't care what—but it had better be thrilling. And I want it to include Dallas and Alexis. These are your stars, and they need a star storyline."

He hit the table with his Montblanc pen the way a judge bangs a gavel. Webster Strong had spoken. I wasn't sure what to say. I looked to Richard.

"That's a great idea, Webster," Richard said.

What was a great idea? He hadn't suggested anything remotely great. It was all recycled cheese.

Richard continued, "Mal and I and the writers will get together and brainstorm. We'll come up with something a little bit spicier for our first episode. We'll reshoot some scenes later this week and lay them in—no problem. Right, Mallory?"

This was it—the moment of truth. But what option did I really have? I knew what Richard was doing: He was getting us away from the table as soon as he could so we could make some changes on our own terms instead of having them dictated by the suits. If I refused to do it, I would seem as immature as they wanted me to be. Threatening cancellation was serious—and I knew Webster wouldn't be able to do it if he didn't have Trip backing him up. I'd confirm it later with Greg, but just from the way he looked, I knew: Trip was in on this. So it wasn't a question of whether anything would change or not—it was just a question of how much. And Richard was trying to give us as much control over that as possible. Or so I had to hope.

"Fine," I said.

Webster Strong and Holly Hughes looked pleased. Too pleased.

"I can't tell you how excited we are about this," Holly said.

"*So* excited," Webster added.

What had I just done?

"You hung me out to dry," I said to Richard as we walked to the writing office.

"You did that all by yourself," he replied. "You didn't need my help at all."

"You're supposed to be on my side."

"No, Mallory—I'm supposed to be on the *show's* side. Although in this case, I did you a favor."

I stopped and glared at him. "How?" I asked. "How exactly did you do me a favor?"

"Because I agreed with them," he answered simply. "Not about the alien babies or even about turning Deception Pass into a hotbed of free love. But the boring part, Mallory. I agree about the boring part. I kept silent, because I knew if I'd agreed with them in there, you would have been majorly outgunned."

"So what do we do now?" I asked, completely deflated.

"Fix it, Mallory. You go in there and fix it."

The plotline of *Likely Story* was meant to be pretty simple: Ryan and Sarah are in love with each other, but things keep getting in their way. So Ryan goes off with Jacqueline (Francesca's character), and Marco immediately moves in and snaps up Sarah. Everybody is with the person he or she shouldn't be with, pining for someone he or she can't have. Basically, realism. Life, I figured, was dramatic enough. Why add alien babies?

As I followed Richard into the writers' room, I had to remind myself that none of these people would be here if it hadn't been for my initial idea. There was no denying, though, that once the show went into production, the idea became much more of a collaboration than I'd ever imagined it would be. I mean, there was no way I could write all of the episodes myself. We needed a staff of writers in order to do five shows a week.

Luckily, I'd been able to hire one of my friends to be on the writing staff. Tamika and I had met in drama camp when I was a kid. She was older—she'd been an eighteen-year-old counselor, which seemed like a woman of the world to a ten-year-old camper like me. She was the only person at the whole camp who respected that I would have rather been sent to the pound than be in the camp's production of *Cats*. Not that there was anything wrong with *Cats* (okay, there was), but I just wanted to be setting the stage rather than walking across it. Her father was a big-time music producer, and she'd therefore been raised in the same off-kilter world of semi-celebrity as I had. She understood that I'd gone to drama camp because the only other option my mother had given me was fat camp. (I wasn't fat; my mother argued that it was "a preventative measure.")

Neither Tamika nor the other seven writers seemed surprised when I told them what had happened in the meeting.

"What was wrong with the original story about Ryan and Sarah's breakup?" asked Rita from the breakdown corner of the room.

We had two different types of word whizzes on the show: breakdown writers and scriptwriters. The BWs were responsible for writing the detailed outlines of each day's episode.

Once those were approved, we passed them along to the scriptwriters, who then spun that magic into dialogue. I, as head writer, was responsible for the overarching stories that drove the show. In other words, I dreamed up the big stuff and the staff filled in the details.

I leaned back in my chair, unconsciously mimicking the same pose and tone Webster had affected earlier. "The brass thinks it's boring. Not splashy enough," I said.

Tamika played with the long scarf wrapped around her neck, twisting the fringe. "How 'bout we stick Dallas and Alexis on the foggy bridge and have them spot a dead body on the black-sand beach below?"

At first, I thought she was joking. But then Rita asked, "Who's dead?" and Tamika said, "Maybe somebody from their school."

A couple of the other writers actually *oohed* at that.

"What do you think, Richard?" I asked. He would put his two cents in eventually, so I figured I might as well get it now.

He didn't even look up from the BlackBerry he was jabbing at with his thumbs. "Everyone likes murder. Worked for *Desperate Housewives*."

A guy named Chase picked it up from there. "Who said it was murder? It could be anything—a real mystery."

"Of course it's murder—it's always murder," Richard said matter-of-factly.

"Do you think this is what the network wants?" I pressed.

"It's a hell of a lot better than a geography test. No one will tune in to watch actors take tests."

"Having a character stress out about a test isn't the same as *watching him take the test*," I argued. Then I realized the fact

41

that I was arguing meant that I had to be losing. "You approved those storylines. Besides, this is what kids do. They
take tests. And tests are a big deal when you're in school."

Richard didn't even have to roll his eyes. I was drowning in
my own quicksand. And I had to admit that he was right:
Everyone *does* like murder. Or at least they do when it's con-
fined to a fictional town.

"Okay," I said. "Let's see where this goes. Who died? A
student? It seems it should be a student because that would
implicate any number of our characters."

Rita bounced her pencil on the pad of paper in front of her.
"What kind of student? A cheerleader?"

Tamika interjected, "That's been done. It's more interesting if she's a bad girl."

Ronald, a doughy scriptwriter I'd salvaged from *Good As
Gold,* spoke up. "Of course she's a bad girl. But if she's all-
American at first, it will give us more to play with. Everyone
thinks she's perfect, but then we begin to peel away the layers
and we discover that she was a bad girl masquerading as a
good girl."

I groaned. This was starting to sound like every story ever
written. "Are you sure this hasn't been done to death? Pardon
the pun."

"For my money, I always like to see some bitch get dead,"
cracked Tamika.

I sighed. "I suppose as long as we agree that whoever killed
this good girl is not suffering from schizophrenia, we should
be fine. No double personalities on this show. I hate double
personalities."

Ronald piped up again. "How about triple? Do you mind *triple* personalities?"

"Triple personalities who fall in love . . . ," Rita said dreamily.

I looked to Tamika to be my one remaining link to sanity.

"One person, one personality," she said firmly.

And so it went as we batted around the idea of a murder in Deception Pass. Eventually, we settled on the idea of a character named Michelle, the student council president, who is found dead. No one knows who did it. And neither did we . . . yet.

"You're not dead," I told her.
"You're the best," she said.

f i v e

The death immediately started to take on a life of its own.

I believe the chain of events went something like this: Richard told the network what we were thinking; the network told Frieda Weiner, the consultant; and then Frieda Weiner, the consultant, decided to consult everybody else on the set about it.

By the time I got to the shoot for the cast photo, you could feel the body count in the air.

The worst thing was, I could tell that most people were actually excited about it. This, they felt, was real drama . . . even if there wasn't anything real about it.

Alexis looked concerned when she came up to me.

"I'm not going to be the one who dies, am I?" she whispered.

"No," I assured her, "you're the lead. We don't kill leads. At least not in the first year."

She exhaled, relieved.

"I don't know how I'd ever explain being killed to my mother," she confided. "She'd be so disappointed in me."

"You're not dead," I told her.

"You're the best," she said. Then she gave me the kind of hug a little girl gives her dad when she discovers a puppy with a birthday ribbon in her stack of presents.

Francesca and Dallas didn't seem as huggy. At least toward me. They didn't say anything until we were posed next to one another for the big group photo.

"Hi, guys," I said as Sal, the photographer, adjusted my stance.

"Hey," Dallas said, but his voice wasn't really into it.

"Dallas has something to ask you," Francesca said. "Isn't that right, Romeo?"

"C'mon, Francesca," he mumbled.

(Francesca, I noticed, was never Fran or Franny or Franc or Cesca. Always Francesca. I wondered whether it would catch on if I started calling her Rances.)

"What is it?" I asked.

"I dunno," he hemmed.

"Romeo?" Francesca prompted.

"Well . . . ," he hawed.

"It's this whole murder thing," Francesca finally said. "We just didn't see the show going in *that* direction."

"No talking!" Sal shouted, then flashed a few bulbs in our faces.

When I got my sight back, Sal shouted, "No blinking this time!" and unleashed a new barrage.

"Man!" I groaned. Then I looked at Francesca and Dallas next to me and Javier and Alexis at their sides. None of the actors had a problem with the blinking thing. How, I wondered, do you learn not to blink?

Finally, when Sal said it was okay to move, I explained, "The murder is something the network wanted."

"Yeah," Francesca said. "But we didn't sign up for the network's show. We signed up for yours."

"It's still mine," I said. "Nothing's happened that I didn't want to happen."

I was wondering what else to say when I noticed my mother had come onto the soundstage, ready for her close-up.

"All right!" Sal announced. "Javier and Francesca, you can go. Alexis, go put on the white dress. Dallas, let's get that shirt off of you."

Dallas looked a little stunned. "What?" he asked.

Sal gestured to Dallas's torso. "The shirt. Take it off." He held up a little spray bottle. "Don't worry—I can make you glisten."

"I think my shirt will stay on," Dallas said. "I don't mind if it's an important part of a scene. But not on a photo shoot."

Richard had now walked in and was standing next to my mom, who was loving every minute of this.

"I'll take off *my* shirt," Javier proclaimed, and proceeded to do so. "There!"

Alexis ran off to wardrobe, no doubt shocked by the whole spectacle.

"You just want to see him with his shirt off, Javier," Francesca said acidly.

"Oh, honey, I've already seen it in wardrobe a hundred times. And let me tell you, he has hair in *all* the right places." He paused. "But then you'd already know that, wouldn't you?"

Okay, this was *way* too much information.

"Let's just keep the shirt on," I said. "I don't think it would make sense for Mom, Alexis, and me to be wearing what we're wearing while we stood next to a bare-chested guy."

Even saying *bare-chested* made me blush.

Sal looked miffed. "Do you have a no-nudity clause in your contract?" he asked.

Dallas shook his head.

My mother chimed in: "More people will watch the show if you take off your shirt."

Alexis—quick-change artist—reappeared in the white dress.

"Just take the pictures," I implored.

"Fine," Sal grumbled, returning to his camera. He didn't look very happy. And neither did Dallas.

What was he thinking?

I had no idea. And that bothered me.

"Who's going to be murdered?" my on-set tutor (I know: lame) asked me.

"Can we stick to trigonometry?" I replied. This was not a request I'd *ever* thought I'd make.

"Suit yourself," Miss Julie said, miffed. I was pretty sure she was only using me as an excuse to be on the set. Usually, they try to screen out any wannabe actors from being tutors. But this woman was a wannabe *viewer*. I had no doubt that every word I said to her would end up on a blog someday. I had quickly discovered that I was better off with Wikipedia than I was when Miss Julie was in a soap-struck haze.

As soon as I could, I headed off to a better teacher—Gina, the woman who'd been my mother's makeup person since before I was born. One of the only saving graces—okay, the *only* saving grace—of having my mom on my show was that she brought Gina along with her.

Gina often knew set gossip before I did. So the recent turn in *Likely Story*'s direction was old news by the time I stopped by my mother's dressing room.

"They always start with murder," she told me. "Have they brought up Shakespeare yet?" I shook my head. "Oh, honey, they will. '*Hamlet* starts with a murder,' they'll say. And *Macbeth*. 'Who are you to argue with Shakespeare?' they'll say. And the murder goes in."

Hearing Shakespeare's name made me think of Francesca calling Dallas *Romeo*.

I decided not to wonder about it. I focused back on Gina.

"Once the murder goes in, they start to use that as an opening for other things. Fights over money. Shipwrecks. Suicide pacts. Mistaken identities. And each time, they can say Shakespeare, until you completely lose your will."

"Nobody's said Shakespeare," I assured her.

"Well, be on your guard anyway."

"And there are no alien babies in Shakespeare, right?"

Gina shrugged. "At this point in my life, I get *Twelfth Night* confused with *Guiding Light*. Who knows?"

This was *not* the pep talk I'd been hoping for. No doubt sensing this, Gina started to rub my back.

"If anyone can do it, I know you can," she reassured me. "You were raised by soaps. You know how it works. Beat 'em at their own game."

I was so exhausted by the time I got home that I don't think I could've beaten an infant at a game of arm wrestling. Mom went straight for the Pom 'n' Goose, while I went straight to my room.

When I turned on my computer, there was an immediate blipping noise—Keith IM'ing me.

rocketboy: hey, ariel.

malcontent: hey, generic Disney prince character whose name I can't remember right now.

rocketboy: eric.

malcontent: really? eric? how do you get from 'prince charming' to 'prince eric'?

rocketboy: dunno. u just getting in?

malcontent: yup. long day.

rocketboy: me too. only got home from cpk a few minutes ago.

rocketboy: who wants to go for a dip in your pool?

rocketboy: I do!

malcontent: I'm afraid I'd only sink if I got near a body of water.

rocketboy: ☹

Now, usually when I see an emoticon, I want to slap it across the face. But this particular sad face just made me feel bad. Keith had just spent six hours working at CPK, carrying crates of shredded mozzarella cheese up from the basement, cleaning up little kids' spilled drinks as their parents yelled at them, and getting assaulted on all ends by cooks and waitstaff who were just as stressed as he was. It made no sense that I was the exhausted one. I didn't need to be on my feet all day. I wasn't in desperate need of the money (most of which I wouldn't get until I turned eighteen). By all rights, I should've been wide awake. But instead, all I could be was sorry.

malcontent: truly, I'd only drown. can we go under the sea another night soon?

rocketboy: just as long as you're still a part of my world.

As soon as we signed off, I was going to log off altogether. But then, even though it had been months since we'd really spoken, I instinctively looked at my buddy list to see if Amelia was on. It used to be that I couldn't end a night until I'd told her about it.

Her screen name, of course, was nowhere to be found. She'd blocked me as soon as we'd rifted. It's amazing how easily a friend can disappear from your life, if she wants to.

I admit: Early on, right after it happened, I would go on under a new screen name, just so I could see if she was on. I never tried to make contact with her or mislead her. I just wanted to see if she was on.

Not tonight, though. Tonight, I would just feel blocked. Shut out.

Our friendship was far beyond my reach.

"Remember," I said coldly, "I didn't ask you to be on this show. You forced your way on."

six

I was jolted awake by the shrill crow of my cell phone at five-thirty the next morning.

"Mallory?" a voice asked when I answered. It took me a moment to realize: Greg. It was Greg's voice.

"Greg?"

"I'm so sorry. I won't even ask, 'Did I wake you?' because then you'd just say no to be polite and I would still feel awful."

"I think I'd say yes, Greg. What is it?"

"I have Trip on the line for you. New York time, you know."

I groaned. "Put him through."

Poor Greg—when Trip was on New York time, he probably had to be in the office at five in the morning. Because God forbid a network executive should ever have to dial direct. . . .

"Mallory!" Trip sounded as artificially bright as a sunlamp. "Just wanted to check in with you—I talked to Webster and Richard, and they filled me in on the murder and the new direction. I just wanted to tell you I think it's a fantastic decision, and I'm sure it will get the show to where we need it to be. If you have any problems whatsoever, just give me a holler—through Greg, of course."

"Well, I . . . ," I started to say.

"Oh, Mallory? I'm afraid my car is here, and I have some calls I have to make in the car. Give my love to your mother. Wait—scratch that. Keep it all for yourself, okay? And good luck today."

I didn't even get the *b* in *bye* out before I had the dial tone. I wanted Greg to come back on the line, but he no doubt had to dial all of Trip's other morning calls.

Once I'm awake, there's no getting back to sleep, so I went over to my computer and tried to write. It was strange, though—now that we had a staff of writers, it wasn't like I could just sit down and make the scripts up on my own. I had to wait my turn, and it had to all fit into the master plan.

"Forget that," I told myself. I would just sit down and write a *Likely Story* scene, whether we ended up using it or not. I decided to write a scene for Ryan and his new girlfriend, Jacqueline. Which meant, of course, I was really writing a scene for Dallas and Francesca.

JACQUELINE
Do you still think about her?

RYAN
Who?

JACQUELINE (*laughing*)
I'll take that as a yes.

RYAN (*sheepish*)
Not much. Every now and then.

JACQUELINE
Why, Romeo? Why?

RYAN
You can't just let go of
someone instantly. They
linger with you. It takes a
long time to get them out of
your thoughts, even if you no
longer see them.

JACQUELINE
Do you think Sarah still
loves you?

RYAN
She's with someone else now.
She has Keith.

JACQUELINE
Keith?

RYAN
I meant Marco.

JACQUELINE
But you said Keith.

                    RYAN
          You're trying to trap me into
                 saying it.

                  JACQUELINE
                 Saying what?

                    RYAN
              That I love . . .

Okay, stop. I had to stop.

I climbed into bed and tried to fall back asleep.

Forty very awake minutes later, I got back out of bed.

"You look horrible!" my mother said as soon as I got to the kitchen.

"Did you even sleep?" I asked her. "Or did you just stay here all night, waiting to deliver that line?"

"You can't look that horrible today of all days! You look like death warmed in a toaster oven!"

I wanted to grab the nearest spatula and do mean things with it. *Death warmed in a toaster oven* was one of the off-kilter phrases the writers had often given Mom's character, Geneva, on *Good As Gold*. She was so lost in her soap opera world that she believed people talked like this in real life, too.

"I haven't even showered yet," I pointed out.

"Well, shower!"

"Can I eat something first?"

"No!"

When I returned to the kitchen, showered and brushed, Mom still looked on edge. We headed to the set together, but before I left for the writers' office, she told me to be ready to go to Gina for a "fix-up" at eleven-thirty.

"Why?" I asked, mystified.

She came up to me and spoke in the low sotto voce she reserved for important news like Daytime Emmy nominations and Q scores.

"We'll be having lunch today at The Ivy."

I knew what this meant: The only reason people ate there was to show other people that they *can* eat there. Evidence: I'd already been there once with Richard.

"I have too much work to do, Mom," I pleaded. "And I've already been to that chow palace of the damned."

"It *is* work," she intoned with a Cleopatra-like seriousness. "Perhaps bigger than we can even dream."

Mother picked up a strand of my tangled hair and said, "This still needs to be fixed. And the outfit—it's nice but not 'pow!' I'll have Gina make this a priority. Be there by eleven-thirty. The reservation is at *one*."

I knew my mother had to be proud of this. Reservations at one were the hardest to get.

"Nice," I said.

"I know. Don't be late."

The wackiness continued when I got to the writers' office.

"Go ask Richard about the sexy teachers," Tamika told me as soon as I walked in. "He's in his office."

So I went straight down the hall to Richard's office. Unlike the writers' office, which was a sprawl of paper and empty Vitaminwater bottles, Richard's was immaculate.

I didn't knock. He didn't seem surprised.

"Good morning, Mallory," he said, pleasantly enough.

"Tell me about the sexy teachers, Richard," I replied.

He didn't miss a beat. "As you've no doubt just heard, the network would like us to add a pair of sexy teachers to the show, and I said yes."

I tried to keep my calm. "How sexy are these teachers going to be, Richard? Will they wear bikinis to class?"

Richard sighed. "First of all, one of them is male, and we're not the kind of show that puts a grown man in a bikini. Second, the idea is for them to be sexy *together*, if you get my drift."

"Richard . . ."

"Look—this is compromise, Mallory. You don't want your characters to be having sex? Fine. But *someone* has to be having sex, and while I would advocate your mother being the one to have sex, I am guessing Trip Carver would have a thing or two to say about that. So that means new characters. New sexy characters who can have the sexless sex preferred on daytime soap operas."

"The sexy teachers will only be having sex with each other, not with the students?"

"Correct."

"I don't like it."

"You don't have to like it. You just have to do it. Annie's already working on the casting."

"I'll talk to the writers," I said, and moved to leave.

Before I could get out the door, Richard told me one more thing.

"Part of getting what you want is knowing how to keep it," he said. "Remember that."

I had little doubt I could forget it now.

The writers seemed jazzed to have some sexy teachers to work with. Apparently, if you're writing five episodes a week, it helps to have more than five significant characters.

I was less jazzed when eleven-thirty came and it was time for me to be "fixed up."

Jim the Wardrobe Boy sat me down on a small folding stool. He started going through racks of clothes and picking out various blouses, mini-dresses, halters, and such.

Finally he found a Betsey Johnson number that was mostly canary yellow but had a small cornflower print that gave it a soft blue under-hue. "Try this," he dictated.

Once the dress was on, I realized Jim knew what he was doing. I looked good—a little young, maybe, but it made my not-so-notable cleavage look like gangbusters. And suddenly I realized I had pretty nice legs. They looked even better when he shoved my feet into Jimmy Choos and I was suddenly four inches taller.

Jim gave me the once-over and clucked with approval. "Fix the hair and you'll kill 'em, Madame Producer." He pronounced *Madame* with a French accent—two loooong, luxurious *ahhh*s.

Kill 'em? Who was I trying to kill?

When I got to the makeup trailer, I asked, "Gina—what the heck is going on with this Extreme Makeover, Mallory Edition? I mean, I know I wasn't exactly *Vogue* Cover Girl of the Month this morning, but still . . . I could've just worn the Marc Jacobs from yesterday if everyone was so concerned."

"There are two reasons for that, Mallory," said Gina as she

worked on my hair like Edward Scissorhands with a meth problem. "One is that you are too young for this Marc Jacobs. I respect your mother's attempt at buying you appropriate levels of fashion for your new position, but she's got some things wrong. This Marc Jacobs is for thirtysomethings who want to *look* sixteen. Not sixteen-year-olds trying to look thirty."

"And this makes me look sixteen?" I asked incredulously.

"We're getting there. . . ." I could hear in her voice that she was leaving normal reality and was becoming a follicle fascist where every hair was a potential revolutionary just waiting to cause havoc and bring down her carefully constructed empire.

I tried to get her attention back. "Gina!" I hollered. "Why am I getting made over like I'm a drab housewife who got lucky on *Oprah*?"

Gina didn't say anything at first. Instead, she scuttled across the ever-shrinking trailer to the wig, fall, and emergency toupee closet, pretending to search for something. You might not think that a teen soap would need an emergency toupee supply, but like the Red Cross with its blood banks, you never know when disaster will strike. Better to be prepared than not for the inevitable day when your main star has decided to shave his head during a drunken night on the Sunset Strip. I learned a few weeks ago during one of the infinity-plus meetings I'd taken that fake hair was a major part of every soap opera's budget. Who knew so many daytime stars suffered from female-pattern baldness?

Since my hair was fine (for now?), it still didn't explain why I was undergoing a drastic makeover, from young upstart exec to starlet lite.

I voiced this again to Gina, and to her credit, she couldn't evade my questions any longer.

"You didn't hear any of this from me—all right?" she said in a hushed tone.

"Gina, of course. Nothing that passes between us would ever become public."

"It's not the public I'm worried about. It's your mother." She came back to my chair and started fussing with my hair again. It was becoming shorter and shorter. "You are not supposed to know, but network publicity has tipped off all the paparazzi in town to the fact that you and your mother will be lunching at The Ivy today. And by 'tipped off,' I mean they've begged, bargained, and blackmailed to get you coverage. The publicists are planning on getting this in every celebrity rag and blog by week's end."

"I have no business in front of the flashbulbs!" I protested. "That's for people like—"

"People like you." Richard's timing was almost eerily perfect. "Sorry to break it to you, sweet cheeks, but you *are* the story. You and your mom are the perfect story. A publicist couldn't dream this up no matter how many Ambien he took and how many hours he slept on his two-thousand-thread-count sheets. Daytime is dying, but you are the Messiah. And to quote Shakespeare, 'A picture is worth a thousand words'— you and your mom together at The Ivy. It couldn't be better if she was passing you the Olympic Torch while you fed starving orphans."

"So now I'm just a pawn?"

"You're not a pawn—you're a ploy," Richard responded calmly. Clearly he had been expecting this. "We wanted you to go unawares so that you'd look natural and young and innocent in front of the cameras. It would be one thing if we wanted to manufacture a feud between you and your mom—we could've taken that angle. But we all decided the torch-passing was a better scenario. It makes you look important and it transitions your mother into the older-woman roles she's now destined to play."

"This was her idea, wasn't it?"

Richard nodded.

I stood up. "It's always about her, isn't it?" I said to Gina. "This is about getting her in the spotlight, not the show."

"Sit down," Richard said.

I didn't.

"Fine. You can take this standing up. I know your whole life you've seen your mother as one of the biggest stars in the universe. But it's a very small universe, Mallory. Soap stars are never A-list, except at soap conventions. They're not like movie stars. They're like made-for-TV-movie stars. Your mother has had to fight for every single mention she's gotten in *People*. She's had to scheme and seduce and spend for every minute on *Entertainment Tonight*. She's getting a burst of attention now because everyone's nostalgic about *Good As Gold* ending. But that won't last. It's a vicious cycle—you can't get power if you can't command attention, and you can't command attention if you don't have power. Am I right, Gina?"

Gina nodded sadly.

"So, yes, Mallory, you're being used here. I'm sorry if it offends you to wear heels, although clearly you love those shoes or else you wouldn't be strutting like an aristocratic peacock right now. You are going to do this for the show, and you are going to do this for your mother. Because we never would've gotten the network publicists to do it for her alone. And she needs the attention. Not just because she's a vain, insecure television actress. But because the attention is her life, Mallory. You of all people should know that. So sit back down so Gina can finish your hair."

Gina, white as a Donna Karan oxford, got back to plying my hair with gels and fudges to give it that certain something. I didn't even care what that something was anymore.

Richard continued, "It's crucial for us to maintain *Good As Gold*'s audience for *Likely Story*. Part of your job is to make that happen. And yes, in a perfect world, the sheer brilliance of your scripts would be enough, but since I doubt they'll be winning any Pulitzers anytime soon, what we really need is FREE PUBLICITY. There are no sweeter words to a network's ear—except maybe *high profit margin*. The point is: You and your mother having lunch at The Ivy means that you are players, that you are buzz-worthy, and that the four corpses who still watch *Good As Gold* will watch your show, too, so help me God. Now put on that mascara and look like a good girl and go eat your sixty-dollar Cobb salad next to every other It girl in town. Smile for all those cameras. Every single one, Mallory. We *need* them."

I was stunned into silence. I'd always resented my mother's publicity demands, but now I saw they were part of the deal. If you wanted people to care about your show, you had to make them care about *you*. Richard was right. This was my job.

I started to sweat in my armpits. *I am not a society girl*, I thought. *I can't do this*. Richard kept glaring at me. I wanted to call Keith right then and tell him to pick me up.

At that moment, Dallas walked into the trailer, looked me up and down, and said, "Hey, great cut." Then he grabbed a Chap Stick from the counter and was gone before I could respond.

I stared at my new reflection in the mirror as a way of avoiding any eye contact with Richard. He sat down in the other chair. Out of habit, Gina began to go at his hair.

"Just a little around the sides, please," Richard told her, as if he was accustomed to having his hair cut at any particular time in any random chair. "Focus on getting the premature gray out if you can. And, Mallory, remember not to fraternize with the actors. It will only cause trouble."

Fraternize? I hadn't even said a word to Dallas! Were my thoughts that obvious?

"I know," I sputtered. "But . . ." I couldn't think of how to finish that sentence.

As I moved to leave, Richard reached out to me like a lazy invalid from his barber's chair.

"You, me—post-lunch. We got some potatoes to hash-brown, if you know what I mean."

I had no idea what he meant. Though just to get out of there, I repeated, "You, me—post-lunch. I'll be so post it'll be post-modern."

"Funny you mention that, Mal," Richard said, relaxed this time because Gina was rubbing his temples. "Post-modernism figures heavily in what we need to discuss. I hope you like it."

Just then, the siren horn of a luxury automobile bleated like a dying lamb and I knew it was too late for me to escape. I stepped outside into the piercing California noonday sun and began my forced march toward Hollywood destiny.

"Who cares?!" my mother repeated indignantly. "The fans care—and you had better start caring about them or else this Love Boat you've got us all sailing on will be sunk before we hit San Diego."

s e v e n

Robertson is one of the main celebrity drags in Los Angeles. While Rodeo Drive is for tourists and just-Botoxed trophy wives too lazy to leave Beverly Hills, Robertson is where "locals" go to overspend on James Perse T-shirts and Cynthia Rowley dresses. It's where starlets like to get into car accidents. A couple of prominent production companies have offices there, but it's essentially dominated by shopping and lunching options. Robertson starts more or less in West Hollywood at Santa Monica Boulevard with a cluster of gay bars and cafés and then slowly becomes more and more dominated by high-end retail shops the farther south you drive. Its beating heart—the main muscle from which all the surrounding glamour flows—is The Ivy.

My mother and I were chauffeured in a vintage silver Rolls past the tiny boutiques, and I had to admit I was somewhat drawn to things I saw in the windows. My mother had always lavished me with expensive clothes and toys, but I'd always resented them because they were a symbol of what she wouldn't provide: nurturing attention and love. But now that

I could potentially afford some of these items myself—with my own money—it made me reconsider (only slightly) the merits of treating oneself to the finest of everything. Someone had to do it, right?

My mother spent most of the car ride scribbling away on a pad. She barely spoke the entire time, which was fine since the driver was playing NPR at my request. Eventually, I had to know what it was she was working on.

"What's that?" I asked.

She put the pad down in her lap and sighed with exhaustion as if she were trying to hammer out the details of a Middle East peace agreement.

"*Soaps Monthly* has asked me to compile a list of my five favorite moments from my many years on *Good As Gold*. It's like trying to pick the five finest Fabergé eggs or the most gorgeous statue at the Louvre. I don't know what to choose."

"What have you got so far? When you narrowly escaped being executed on death row? When your plane caught fire and you narrowly escaped being killed in the crash? Or when you single-handedly discovered the cure that saved Max from being killed by the flesh-eating bacteria?"

"No," she said, waving her hand dismissively at me, "those are all so obvious. Number one is of course the birth of Diamond."

"Really?" I blushed. It never occurred to me that the birth of Geneva's daughter, which matched my birth in real life, would be that meaningful to her.

"Naturally—it was one of the highest-rated storylines in *Good As Gold*'s history!"

Oh, right—it had nothing to do with me, just the ratings. "Then what else is on the list?" I said with diminishing interest.

"I'm thinking about the time I was forced to work as a high-priced hooker in order to get Diamond the new kidney she needed. Also maybe when I risked jail by perjuring myself on the stand in order to save Rance from the gas chamber because I knew it was Roger, not Rance, who'd killed Ricardo in a drunken rage at Charlotte's wedding reception. But I couldn't reveal *that* because I thought I was carrying Roger's love child."

"Those are fine. Just pick anything—who cares?" I said, looking out the window at the girls with Chihuahuas in their purses strolling up and down the sidewalks.

"Who cares?!" my mother repeated indignantly. "The *fans* care—and you had better start caring about them or else this Love Boat you've got us all sailing on will be sunk before we hit San Diego."

"Remember," I said coldly, "I didn't ask you to be on this show. You forced your way on."

She put a hand on my leg and said, "That's called being an opportunist, and you'd best learn a thing or two about it or you'll find yourself without a job and, God forbid, without royalties. I won't have you living in my basement forever like some stoner garage-band bass guitarist."

"Don't worry, Mom, I'll be out of your hair and your house the day I turn eighteen. Count on that."

This seemed to wound my mother more than I expected. Instead of retorting with a nasty comment, she looked slightly stricken and remained silent. I could hear Gina *tsk*ing sadly in

73

my head: Why couldn't I be nicer to my mother? Richard's words started to haunt me; I had to remember that my mother needed this as much as the show did. It was a hard adjustment to make—I had always thought of my mother as the biggest star in the galaxy. What kid doesn't, whether her mother is a flight attendant or a nurse or a librarian or a soap actress? As much as I hated it when she threw her invulnerability at me, it was even worse to think of her as vulnerable. I had never gotten used to the fact that I had to rely on her. And now, to be told she was relying in some way on me . . . that made me feel much more like a grown-up than any outfit ever would.

We pulled up to The Ivy, and suddenly the sidewalk and street were swarming with locusts. Dressed in various flannels and denims, these shutterbugs were outside every window of the car. Thankfully, the windows were tinted.

"This is insane!" I said as my heartbeat quickened. "I've never seen anything like this before. I mean, from the inside." The network publicists must have pulled a lot of favors—or spent a lot of money—on this.

My mother coiffed her hair in the window reflection. She opened her purse and put on her favorite pair of Chanel sunglasses. Then she took out a small box decorated with a bow and handed it to me.

"Welcome to Hollywood, dear. I think you'll be needing these."

I unwrapped the present. It was a gorgeous pair of Chrome Hearts sunglasses. Tortoiseshell with wood inlay. This local brand (i.e., based in LA rather than Milan, Paris, New York, or Taiwan) was all that and a bottle of Dom Pérignon.

"These are beautiful, Mom, but they must have cost a fortune."

She grinned wickedly. "Of course, and all the paparazzi out there know it. They couldn't even afford the valet parking fees at Sunset Plaza, where I got them."

"Thank you."

"Now put them on—the siren call of fame and fortune is beckoning!"

The driver opened the car door and my mother emerged. She posed and waved and smiled and turned to this side and that, all the while trying to look like the entire brouhaha was a complete surprise and that she had absolutely no idea anyone would be taking photos that day. Then she stuck her hand back into the car and pulled me out. A sudden lightning storm of flashbulbs went off all around us.

My mother yelled out over the din, "This is my gorgeous and completely genius daughter, Mallory, with whom I'll be working on the greatest new program daytime television has seen in decades: *Likely Story!*"

I hate to be so banal as to say I was like a deer in the headlights, but it was totally like that at first. Then, after just a moment in which my eyes adjusted, I realized I didn't mind the attention. I grinned, I waved, and I tried to look thin. Then I took my mother's hand—something I don't think I'd done since I needed help crossing the street. For a moment, her face turned from Hollywood to human; her smile seemed a little more genuine. She squeezed my hand a second, then led me forward.

The driver started tossing paparazzi out of the way as if they were the defensive line of the New York Giants. My mother tugged me along behind her in the narrow path the driver was creating toward The Ivy's entrance. Behind us the photographers closed back in around us. Then, before I could really get used to what was happening, we were inside the restaurant and it was calm again. A piano tinkled somewhere in the background. Mom let go of my hand.

The room was full of the dull drone of lunchtime chatter. A few heads turned to check us out, but not many. Those who did certainly didn't register any recognition. Even if they did know who my mother was, it was considered a faux pas in LA to ever acknowledge a celebrity's presence.

My mother and I were seated at a small table for two. It wasn't in the best part of the restaurant—it was a bit too close to the kitchen for my mother's taste—but it wasn't the boondocks, either. I had a lobster salad and my mother mostly sipped whiskey sours while she picked at her rib-eye steak, placed delicately on a bed of arugula with feta cheese and cherry tomatoes.

We didn't say much. Though she had expertly maneuvered her way off *Good As Gold* and onto *Likely Story,* I think she was quite sad to see her legacy get canceled so abruptly. Laugh as I did at the horrific storylines and unbelievable situations she "acted" her way through, for the first time I was beginning to understand just how hard she had to work. My mom was on the job before 8 a.m. five days a week and usually worked at least twelve hours on the set. On television, it doesn't look that hard to have a fabulous wardrobe and kiss gorgeous men, but the time it takes to get to those moments is grueling.

By the time I'd sipped my way through my third bottle of

Perrier, I suggested to my mother that we leave. She glanced at her Cartier watch, inlaid with emeralds for every hour. It had been a present from Trip, a memento of their short-lived marriage.

"I guess you're right." She sighed, pushed around her lunch a couple more times for good measure, and then motioned to the waiter for the check. When he brought it over, she dropped a platinum credit card that the network paid for.

The check came back and my mom tipped thirty percent—when it's expensed to the network, why not look generous?

As we approached the exit, my mother grabbed my hand—less spontaneous than before, almost a kind of desperate grab. I didn't know if she was holding on to me for dear life or if she was trying to brace me for the onslaught of photographers outside. The nervous energy passing between us was palpable. My mom was an aging soap star desperately trying to hold on to her past. I was an out-of-my-league example of nepotism at its finest. But we wanted everyone "out there" to forget about those realities and buy the fantasy that our life was exactly that: a fantasy.

Smartly, my mother had summoned the car so it was waiting for us when we stepped outside. Another barrage of flashbulbs exploded in our faces. This time Mom seemed to view it as a wake—a final chance for her spotlight. Rather than milk it, she moped through it, looking down at her Gucci boots as she pressed through the throng.

Once she had climbed back into the Rolls, a reporter shouted out a question to me. I had no idea what he'd asked, so I smiled demurely and said loudly, "Find out on *Likely Story*."

Inside the car, I kicked off the torturous heels and slumped into the tan leather seat. Now it was time to face the second (or was it third? fourth?) gauntlet of the day. Because at that moment, my mother said, "Oh, yes—I almost forgot! We have to drop you off at school!"

"Were you always this much of a bitch?" I asked.
"Only to those who deserve it," she shot back.

e i g h t

In Hollywood, there are strict limits on underage work. This prevents production of *The Mickey Mouse Club* from being a sweatshop. Children under eighteen are not allowed to work more than nine hours on a given day, and they must attend an average of three hours of school per day.

Once a week, I had to stop by my real high school to pick up the week's assignments. I either had to complete them on my own or ask Miss Julie for help.

I glanced at my watch. It was almost three o'clock, right when school would be getting out. Ever since the fallout with Amelia, I usually scheduled these trips either in the morning, when I knew she'd be in class, or long after class had let out so the campus would be a ghost town. But today's mixture of generic LA traffic and my hectic to-do list made such careful planning impossible. I was lucky I had the time to stop by school at all, let alone do the work.

I texted Keith to see if he was still around. Seniors had a smaller class load and got to leave early. He texted back with a negative. CPK owned his soul for the afternoon. I next texted my soapfan friend Scooter, who said he'd come running to meet me as soon as class was over.

I was a bit embarrassed to be pulling up to school in a Rolls. If word got back to Amelia—and I had no doubt it would—it would only confirm her viper view of me.

"Back in a minute, Mom," I said, slipping back into my shoes.

She muttered something but was far too engrossed in her iPhone to form any real words.

I ran tiptoe (the easiest way to negotiate asphalt and heels) across the quad toward the fey Spanish-style building that housed the school's administration. The assistant principal's secretary would have a packet of my assignments waiting for me. Every now and then I would run into one of the other four or five kids at our school who also worked in The Biz. Most of them were on second-rate sitcoms or Nickelodeon shows. Some of them looked superior when they walked the halls, and others looked guilty. I wondered which one I looked like.

I was back on the quad when the final bell rang. A rushing stream of students poured from all the doors surrounding the green. I scanned them quickly to see if I knew any of them. I didn't. They must have been from other grades. But I wondered if I would even recognize anyone in my grade anymore—it had been months since I'd been going to school like a normal person, and I'd only been at this school for a year before that.

"Mallory!" was shouted out across the grass. I breathed a sigh of relief when I saw it was Scooter.

"Hey, Scooter," I said, smiling.

He bounded up to me and enveloped me in a hug. "What are you doing here?"

I waved the packet in my hand. "Just being a good little schoolgirl."

"I'm so jealous." Scooter pouted. "You get to spend all day on a soap set and I'm stuck discussing the fire imagery in *Fahrenheit 451*."

"Trust me, Scoots, I'd trade places in a minute."

"Somehow I doubt that, Mal. Just let me fawn."

He was right, of course. I wouldn't have traded places with him, but I wanted to believe that I could have. It always annoyed me when celebrities begged to be treated like normal people when they'd worked their whole lives to be anything but normal. Not that I was a celebrity by any stretch. Despite the events at The Ivy, I *was* a normal person, in abnormal circumstances. This opportunity had fallen into my lap and I had taken advantage of it. It would have been silly not to. But it was hardly as if I'd gone *looking* for such a chance. Sometimes you just have to say yes to the universe.

"Daughter dearest!" came a shrill cry from the car. A chill ran down my spine. Does every daughter feel that when her mother calls? I doubt it.

"Is that her? Geneva?" Scooter asked in the kind of hushed tone people use for the Dalai Lama or Barbra Streisand.

"She's only Geneva for one more week. *Good As Gold* goes off the air on Friday."

Scooter looked like one of the boys in those novels with dead dogs. "I know," he said mournfully. "I'm totally devastated. I cry at the end of every episode."

I patted Scooter on the head as my mother called for me again. I turned around and yelled back, "Hold your horses! I'm coming!" Then I returned my gaze to Scooter. "Want to meet her?"

"I couldn't possibly," Scooter said nervously, turning beet red.

"Oh, come on, if I can *live* with her, you can *meet* her." I grabbed his hand and pulled him along toward the Rolls.

Inside the car, my mom was paging through the afternoon's shooting script. I motioned for her to roll the window down.

"Mom, I want you to meet my friend Scooter."

She smiled weakly, clearly disinterested. Forever gracious, though, she extended her hand through the window.

Scooter gave it a light shake. "I'm a huge fan, ma'am."

My mother's mood brightened visibly. "Oh, really?" she purred.

"Oh, yes, I've been watching you for as long as I can remember. I couldn't sleep for a week after you snuck onto the UFO to rescue Diamond. I must have been five. You were so brave."

"What a charmer this one is," my mother said to me. "You always bring your sullen, morose friends over to the house. You never bring promising young gentlemen like this one."

I declined to tell her that Scooter had been to the house a handful of times. She'd just been at work. Or passed out.

"I'll try to remember that," I said. "Anyway, we should get going."

"So soon?" my mother asked coyly. "Scooter and I were just getting acquainted."

I wanted to tell her it was pointless to flirt with the gay

boys. But then I realized, no, it was actually the gay boys who loved the flirting the most.

"It's been very nice to meet you, ma'am," Scooter said, his smile floating like a rainbow cloud.

My mother returned the smile. "You know, I'm having a small garden get-together on Friday afternoon to celebrate the last episode of *Good As Gold*. Why don't you stop by? It'll be a magic moment."

Scooter shot me a glance and I shrugged. He stammered an affirmative.

I didn't even know we were having a party. But then, why would I? I suppose, in some ways, I was indirectly responsible for the cancellation of *Good As Gold*.

I hugged Scooter goodbye and walked to the other side of the Rolls. And that's when the phantom menace appeared: Amelia.

I almost dove into the car and yelled, "Drive!" to the chauffeur like an action-movie reject, but instead I stiffened my back and stood up taller in my heels. *Like an aristocratic peacock,* I heard Richard say.

"Hello, Amelia," I offered.

"Hello," she replied.

Was this going to be the start of a real conversation? Was that too much to hope for?

Apparently, yes.

"Slumming it at school, I see," Amelia sneered, sipping coyly from a can of Welch's grape soda.

"How many times do I have to say I'm sorry?"

"That can't erase it, Mallory. This isn't one of your scripts. You don't have any control of the story."

"I know. . . ."

Amelia turned to the Rolls. "Nice car," she said. Then she started to pour grape soda on it.

"What is this, third grade?" I asked.

"No," Amelia said. "*This* is third grade." And then she changed the direction of the can and threw grape soda all over me.

"Oops," she added.

I was dumbfounded. I stood there silently, dripping purple, for what seemed like hours but was surely only seconds.

"Were you always this much of a bitch?" I asked.

"Only to those who deserve it," she shot back.

I opened the door of the car. "I'll see you at the dance," I said. "That is, if you can even find a date for Valentine's Day."

"I have someone who doesn't already *have* a girlfriend, you lying slut," she replied.

"Who? Your slimeball brother, Jake?"

"Ha!" she cried. "I'm going with Brewster Robbins. You know, the lacrosse star you used to lust after."

"That's exciting. You'll be his fifteenth girlfriend this month."

"You are so out of line." She turned and stalked away, waving her middle finger at me from behind her back.

I slammed the car door and looked at the grape-stained Betsey Johnson.

"Friend of yours?" my mother asked drolly.

"Not anymore," I said. And I meant it.

"There's only one way out—through my bedroom."

n i n e

I couldn't believe I had to go back to work, but my days didn't end when the final school bell rang. Back at the lot, my mother quickly ensconced herself in the makeup trailer in order to be ready for her counseling scenes later. I've never seen a high school counselor wear as much eyeliner as my mom's version did, but I guess if we were going to have sexy teachers, a vampy guidance counselor would fit right in.

My phone buzzed with a text reminding me to go see Richard in his office. I found him finishing the last of his California rolls, dabbing them in the wasabi and soy sauce with his plastic chopsticks. *Good As Gold* was playing on the plasma TV in his office, along with a live feed of the *Likely Story* footage being shot on the stage. He didn't look up when I walked in.

"How was The Ivy?" he asked, still not looking up.

"How do you think?" I said, grabbing a Red Bull from the mini-fridge.

"I'm hoping it was a madhouse."

"You are correct, sir," I replied, exhaustion catching up with me.

"Good—at least something's going right today." Richard flicked his soy sauce packets into the trash can and swiveled to face me.

"Something else is flying south besides my life and my patience?"

"Did you spill something?"

"What?" I asked, not following.

He indicated my dress with his chopstick and suddenly I remembered I was wearing most of Amelia's grape soda. "Oh, right. Don't worry, it happened after The Ivy. I ran into my old friend Amelia."

Richard clucked. "Grape is an awfully hard flavor to get out. Next time you get in a squirting match, can you make sure the other girl's drinking Sprite?"

I *so* didn't want to talk about this. "What else has gone wrong since I left for lunch?" I asked.

"I'm not going to say anything to impede your impartial judgment," he went on.

"My judgment about what?" I wondered.

"The opening credits for the show. I just got the cut from the editors."

The opening credits were all-important in establishing the overall mood of the show. *Days of Our Lives* has the iconic hourglass. *The Young and the Restless* was made unforgettable by its plaintive piano theme. *Dallas* had oil and, well, Dallas.

I was hoping for an opening hybrid somewhere between the helicopter shots of *Dallas* and the spooky undertone of *Twin Peaks*. The fact that Deception Pass actually existed up near the tip of Washington State was especially weird. I hadn't realized this when I came up with the name originally, though

I think a fifth-grade geography report on Washington might have planted it in my brain somewhere.

The good news was that it ended up adding tons of texture to my story. Filled with foggy bridges and thick evergreen forests, the real Deception Pass provided a great backdrop for the goings-on of the characters in *Likely Story*. We didn't have the budget to shoot there all the time, but a few well-placed shots of rushing waters and dark coves would hopefully convince the audience that Sarah, Jacqueline, Marco, and Ryan weren't on a soundstage two miles southeast of Burbank, California.

Richard clicked play on the DVD remote and the credits began to roll. I knew we were in trouble by the opening strains of the electric guitar. Electric guitar is *never* a good sign.

First there was a shot of a lighthouse. Kind of intriguing. Then there was Alexis in a bikini getting out of the frigid winter waters of Washington. Her close-up revealed blue lips. Dallas was in a wet suit pulled down to his waist with a surfboard. *His character doesn't surf,* I thought. And we all knew now where Dallas stood on the issue of shirtlessness. Then there was a shot of crabs crawling on a foamy rock. Eww. Crabs were not what I was trying to project. Javier as Marco combed his hair in a mirror. Check minus—that was more likely the real Javier primping than his rugged character. And finally Francesca was seen fixing her car, covered in grime. It was followed by a shot of some random tree and then a quick cut of my mother looking pleased with herself in the guidance office. One more random tree shot . . . and then the screen went black.

"What the hell was that?" I choked out.

"Your show. Should I ask what you thought?"

"That has nothing to do with my show!" I screamed. "Since when does Francesca fix *cars*?!? And don't even get me started on the surfboards and bikinis. This takes place in the Pacific Northwest, not the OC! Oh my God, I'm hyperventilating."

Richard tossed me the paper bag his sushi lunch had arrived in. I started huffing into it and shrieking, "I'm going to kill you, Richard!"

He put up his hands in self-defense and said, "Stick your knife somewhere else, because I am not at fault."

"Then who?" I hissed, finally regaining control over my breathing.

"I think neither you nor I really paid enough attention to this," he said.

"I told them to keep it *real*. Like you can see your own drama reflected in it, especially if you live near Seattle. There's not even a shot of the bridge—the two-pronged amazing bridge that we replicated at great expense on Stage Four."

"Stop yelling. I get it. I hate it, too."

I stopped yelling. "You do?"

"Of course. That tired old indie garage band they have over the credits. That song sucks *now*—in twenty years it will be a laff riot."

"Twenty years? We won't make it twenty minutes at this rate. We've got to reshoot it. And this time I'm going. I won't have all my hard work ruined in thirty seconds of MTV backwash."

"We debut a week from Monday," Richard said. "When are we going to reshoot?"

"This weekend."

Richard was quiet. He toyed with his pencil. "I'll get back to you. In the meantime, you have a photo shoot to get ready for."

"*Another* photo shoot?" How were we going to tape a TV show if people kept taking our photos?

"This time it's *Entertainment Weekly,* which covers daytime TV about as often as it covers greyhound racing. So if someone tells you to smile, you ask, 'How wide?'"

"Just get me new opening credits and I'll smile so wide you'll be able to use it as a hammock," I promised.

Richard raised his eyebrow at that.

"It's starting to be a pleasure to work with you," he said.

Jim the Wardrobe Boy was none too pleased when I returned to his lair with a stained dress. "I lent you a piece of heaven and you brought back a dishrag!" he caterwauled upon seeing me.

I shrugged and apologized halfheartedly. I was too upset with the barf-o-riffic opening titles and nervous about "sexing up" the first couple of episodes to be worried about one ruined Betsey Johnson dress.

For the photo shoot, Jim dressed me in a Marlene Dietrich–style lady tuxedo. I kind of looked like a drag king, but it did make me look tall and important. I liked wearing the pants. Just as I was finishing up in wardrobe, Francesca waltzed in.

"Hi, boss!" she said in a deliberately chipper tone.

"Hi," I replied as I tried to examine my backside in the mirror without perfect girl noticing.

"So I got the new pages a few minutes ago," she said.

I stopped looking at my butt. "What new pages?"

"The episode one reshoot. Where Ryan and Sarah find the student's body. And then Marco and I decide to join them in finding the killer," Francesca explained as she stepped into a periwinkle prom dress.

"Do you have them?" I asked, blood rushing to my face. How dare Richard release new pages without my approval!

"Right here," she said, tossing the stapled packet of xeroxed script toward me.

I flipped through the pages and burned with anger. I hadn't approved any of this slop. Richard had some 'splainin' to do. But first I'd test the temperature of the political waters.

"Francesca, you've read these—what do you think?"

She clicked her tongue against her teeth, clearly searching for a diplomatic answer. "I think they're interesting . . . ," she began. "Different, that's for sure. But maybe we needed something a little more . . . you know . . ."

"No. What?"

"A little more . . . edgy."

"Please interpret. Does that mean you like them?"

"I like edgy as much as the next girl, but I didn't say I liked the pages," she hurriedly replied. Then she backed up. "But, you know, I'm just a private in this army. You say 'march' and I'll march."

I nodded, soaking it in. So she didn't like them, but wasn't about to go on record saying so. Then she looked around, as if she was about to divulge a big secret, and motioned for me to come closer.

In a tone just above a whisper, she said, "I think Dallas is a little more upset."

"How much more upset?" I asked.

"A lot more. And I wouldn't normally say anything, but as a member of this army, I think I should. Just so you know."

I couldn't tell what Francesca's angle was. I assumed it was true—she had to know I was going to ask Dallas about it. But why tell me like this?

"Thanks for letting me know," I said, keeping it cordial.

"I said too much. This stays between us, all right?"

I nodded . . . but as soon as I was out the door, Dallas was the only thing on my mind.

I couldn't lose him.

Things were about to get dirty in this
dry-clean-only town.

t e n

I had to try and put out the Dallas fire without burning the bridges I had carefully constructed with the writers and even Richard. I'd barely read the new pages, but I knew from the lines "That dead girl is my half sister" and "What's this creepy clown mask doing here?" that the scene wasn't heading down Believability Road.

I could only assume that Dallas was already at the photo shoot on the soundstage. Dressed in my lady tux, I deducted that the final "concept" for the shoot had been "Prom." No doubt, this had been a subject of conversation in several meetings over the last several weeks. Magazine shoots don't just accidentally end up materializing like june bugs or the flu. They are the careful, prissy product of several highly paid professionals whose sole job beyond light-meter reading is to decide "concepts."

Thus, I was in a lady tux, the girls in foofy dresses, and the boys . . .

I turned a corner and saw the boys were in tuxedo jackets with shorts. Oy. Tuxedo shorts were a particular atrocity perpetrated upon unsuspecting SoCal students. Every year, some tuxedo rental house would pay male seniors to wear tuxedos around the school to promote their store. Inevitably, these boys would wear the jackets, bow ties, and cummerbunds paired with black board shorts, creating a look that was as uniquely unappealing as it was embarrassing. But seventeen-year-old boys, surprisingly, did not pick up on this . . . leading a handful of mortified prom-picture-taking girls to beg the photographer to only shoot from the waist up. And if the shorts weren't bad enough, the boys usually wore mandals, too.

As I gazed upon the photo-shoot horrors in front of me, I noticed that Dallas and Javier were wearing those old-fashioned kind of socks one usually saw in a stuffy British art-house movie. You know, the kind of socks that are held up by a garter belt below the knee? Not exactly fashionable.

What was even worse was that I saw a throne off to one side. I knew, without a shadow of a doubt, that I was going to be expected to sit on that throne.

"Okay, I think we got it!" bellowed Tai, the blond photographer. She circled her finger in the air to indicate that it was time for a new setup.

As the photo assistants and PAs ran around readjusting lights and props, I sidled up to Dallas and Javier.

"Nice shorts, boys."

Javier rolled his eyes and mimed choking on his own vomit. It was almost as subtle as his acting. Dallas avoided eye contact.

"Got a minute?" I asked.

He looked up from the issue of *Variety* he was paging through and nodded.

"What's up?" he asked when we'd gotten out of hearing range of everyone else.

"I just wanted to check in with you. Make sure everything is okay. Is everything okay?"

He shrugged.

"Is that a yes, no, or maybe?"

"Eh."

"Have you read the new script pages?" I asked, fairly sure of the answer.

He fiddled with the garter on his calf, scratching at the little hairs sandwiched beneath.

"What did you think?" I pressed.

"Maybe this isn't the best place to talk about it."

"Is there a problem?"

He sighed and looked around. "Look, I know you work harder than anybody here. And far be it from me to judge, but these pages are kind of . . . weak. I mean, a clown mask left behind at a crime scene? I think the *Scream* movies are great, but I didn't think that's what we were doing on this show."

"It's not. I didn't write, or approve, these new pages. And trust me, Richard is going to get a big, fat, Greek piece of my mind."

"I am, am I?" Richard said.

Damn him! What was his eerie warlock power to be everywhere at once? I'd have to learn how to do it myself. In the meantime, I knew I was fighting for Dallas's trust . . . so I couldn't back down.

"Yes, you are, Richard. You know nothing gets distributed without crossing my desk first."

"Mallory, we simply don't have time for all these formalities," he replied.

"These pages are junk."

"Your friend Tamika wrote them, not me. That's why I went ahead and had them printed. She's your right hand in the writers' room. I assumed you told her what to do."

I was surprised to hear this. Lines like "Anyone in this town could be a killer" didn't seem like Tamika's style. But I wasn't going to let this blindside me. I was going to stand my ground. For the show. For Dallas. For me.

"I don't care if Anton Chekhov wrote it. I have *not* approved it. And the actors aren't pleased, either."

Richard took out a piece of Nicorette gum and began to chew furiously. "This is not a discussion to be had in front of talent."

This was exactly the wrong time for Dallas to step in. So, of course, this was the moment Dallas stepped in.

"I know that this probably isn't my place . . . ," he began.

"You're right. It's not," said Richard.

"But," Dallas continued as he removed his boutonniere with fierce determination, "I'm going to say this anyway. I'm not going to stand by and watch the show I signed on for get turned into just another daytime soap."

"Listen here, Dallas." Richard popped another piece of Camel gum into his mouth, barely containing his rage. "As an East Coast snob, you might prefer a certain style of Public Television BBC snoozefest storytelling. But here on the West

Coast, we don't want a slice of life; we want a big, hot pie full of drama! I don't know about you, but I also like watching *things happen*. Now, I admit, this murder storyline is a little cliché. . . ."

"A *little*?" I interjected.

"Hey, soap princess, zip it," he said with such firmness that I shut up like a Catholic schoolgirl in the principal's office. "As I was saying, maybe this murder thing is a bit cliché—but what I'm really saying is this is the bomb under the table."

"There's a bomb under the table?" Dallas asked, confused.

"Hitchcock's famous rule was that if you put a bomb under the table at the beginning of a scene, the audience will wait on pins and needles to see if it goes off. By adding the murder mystery at the top of the show, the audience will wait around while Ryan takes Jacqueline car-shopping to see who did it. We're not changing everything; we're just changing a few things in order to make everything else better."

"Richard," I said, trying to remain calm, "I totally agree with you that we need to maybe add a dash of paprika in order to spice things up. But these new scenes are so cheesy and full of holes they'd embarrass the Swiss. Just give me the rest of today and tonight to look things over and make some changes. I'll come up with something better. Something that both you and Dallas like."

Richard spit his gum into his hand and mashed it between his fingers. "Sorry, too late. We've already started taping. We should be able to get it all in the can this afternoon, once everyone's out of the formal wear."

I was thunderstruck. This was absolutely insane! I turned red and yelled, "You can't go over my head like this!"

"I'm the executive producer, and if you'd bothered to familiarize yourself with the chain of command, you'd realize that I have final authority to put pages into production. You are important, Mallory, but ultimately the whole thing hangs on *my* head!"

Dallas jumped in. "That's the problem, Richard. I signed on to do Mallory's show, not yours. I'd rather quit than sit around while you ruin *Likely Story*."

"You can't!" I blurted out, desperate to stop this madness.

"You're exactly right, Mallory," Richard said. "He can't."

"What?" I said.

"Excuse me?" Dallas added.

"I have something up in my office filing cabinets called 'Dallas Grant's Contract.' And that signed piece of paper says that you are mine for the next five years. You can't get out of it without ruining your career. It's airtight. So, if I were you, I'd thank my lucky stars that your producer is not going to hold this outburst against you. Tempers flare. Emotions run high. This is television, not a moonlight drive through Malibu. But if you don't get back to work and keep those pecs harder than a blood diamond, you will find yourself in a coma so fast you won't know what hit you. Don't think I won't do it. I will make you come to work every day for the next five years just to lie in a hospital bed. And then, after five years, I will activate the renewal clause in your contract, even if I have to pay for it myself, so that I get to keep you here two more years. At which time I will make you show up and make you act in a closed coffin so that you forever remember that your career is just as dead as your character. So before you go around upsetting your very talented and very stressed-out head writer any more, I would think long and hard about what exactly your problems really are."

With that, Richard turned on his Prada-loafered heel and walked away.

Dallas and I just stood there, stunned. I had never seen this side of Richard before, not full throttle. But I guess I'd never seen a star threaten to quit before, either.

Finally, I sighed, turned to Dallas, and said, "It's times like these I wish I drank whiskey."

"Ah hear ya, pardner."

A swish of periwinkle came into view, calling, "Romeo, O Romeo! Wherefore art thou Romeo?" Then Francesca saw us and said, "This is the ten-minute call."

"Francesca, don't," Dallas said, his whole body tensed.

"Don't what?" she asked.

"It's not the time."

"Not the time for what, Romeo?"

"STOP IT!" he yelled. Then he turned it on himself. "I. can't. deal. with. this. right. now."

Before Francesca could say another word, he was up and away, leaving the two of us in his wake.

We looked at each other awkwardly.

"I'll go and see what's wrong," I said.

I left before she could stop me.

"Mallory . . . ," he said quietly.

"Yes," I whispered back.

"You can't let this change anything."

e l e v e n

Dallas wasn't hard to find. My first guess was that he'd be in his dressing room. And, sure enough, there he was.

It was barely a room—more like a closet. But the simple fact that he didn't have to share meant the network was expecting big things from him. He was sitting in the room's only chair, with his back to the big mirror on the wall. The door wasn't even closed. I found him staring off into space. When I walked in, he glanced at me, then turned back away. I closed the door.

"Talk to me," I said.

He shook his head. "I can't."

I looked at all the photos he'd hung up around the mirror—all his New York friends, gathered around fountains or performing on the stage. He looked so happy with them.

I pulled over a crate and sat across from him.

"Come on, Dallas. This isn't just about the script, is it?"

He looked at me like I'd just come up with a brilliant insight. He looked at me, and I couldn't tell how he was seeing me. As the boss? As the writer? As a friend? As a girl?

There was no way to know.

I wanted to put my hand on his shoulder. I wanted to tousle his hair. I wanted to touch his cheek and say everything was going to be okay.

But I couldn't. Because I wasn't just seeing him as a friend. I was also seeing him as an actor on my show. I was seeing him as someone on the verge of quitting. And, yes, I was seeing him as a boy. A boy I wanted to like me.

"What just happened with Francesca? What was that about?"

Dallas shook his head again. "It wasn't fair. I shouldn't have snapped at her like that. I just couldn't take it anymore."

"Take what?"

When he didn't say anything, I took a guess and said, "It's the Romeo thing, isn't it?"

He nodded sadly. I was treading on heartbroken ground here.

The next words had to be chosen very carefully.

"So . . . is she . . . your Juliet, then?"

Now Dallas looked confused. "What do you mean?" he asked.

"I mean . . . are you her Romeo?"

Dallas finally got what I was getting at. And he laughed.

"No! I mean, we used to be together. And there's always a chance we'll get back together again—we tend to do that. But that's not what this is about."

"What is it about, then?" I pressed.

And just like that, he shut down again.

"I can't tell you," he said.

"Why not?"

"I can't even tell you that."

"Dallas . . . please. We have to talk about this."

And suddenly there was a voice in my head. A completely unhelpful voice, saying, *He's in love with you.* Francesca called him Romeo when I was around. Was she saying that *I* was his Juliet?!?

My heart started to beat faster. I could see Dallas struggling with it in his head. Knowing he had to say something. Wanting not to say it. But really wanting to say it. Deciding to say it.

What had I gotten myself into? Was I ready for this?

"Mallory . . . ," he said quietly.

"Yes," I whispered back.

"You can't let this change anything."

"It won't."

"It's just that I . . ."

"Yes?"

"This is so hard to tell you."

"Tell me."

"It's like . . . do you know Shakespeare in the Park?"

Now it was my turn to look confused. Was this a metaphor?

He went on. "Shakespeare in the Park? In New York? Joe Papp started it?"

"Yes?" *Mental note: Find out who on earth Joe Papp is.*

"Well . . . before I left Juilliard, I did this, uh, showcase. And the director of this year's production was there. He really liked me. And they're doing *Romeo and Juliet.*"

I still wasn't getting it entirely, but mostly it was my disappointment blocking my comprehension.

"They asked me to be Romeo," he blurted out. "Even after I took this show. He says I'm the perfect Romeo. They think Meryl Streep might be Juliet's nurse and Kevin Kline might be the friar."

He looked so excited for a moment. Then his expression shut down again.

"But of course I can't do it," he said. "I have to be here."

Now the voice inside my head was saying, *He is not in love with you,* and, *How silly of you to think that,* and, *You're holding him back.*

"Look," he said, reaching out and taking my hand. "I want to be here. Truly. I knew what I was getting into when I signed that contract. *Your* show. I'm willing to stay for that. It's the rest of it that's confusing me."

"It's confusing me, too," I confided.

There was suddenly a knock on the door.

"They need you at the photo shoot, Dallas!" one of the PAs yelled.

He let go of my hand and stood up. I stood up, too.

"Hey," he said, gesturing to our ridiculous clothes, "we match!"

"Yeah," I said, looking him in the eye, "we match."

And that awful, unhelpful voice in my head said, *Maybe . . .*

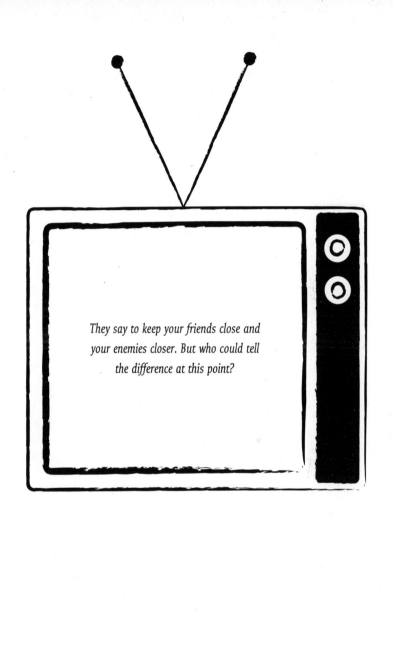

They say to keep your friends close and your enemies closer. But who could tell the difference at this point?

t w e l v e

Needless to say, the photo shoot that followed was anything but fun. The minute Dallas saw Richard there, he became totally withdrawn, his mood ranging from suppressed fury to abject despair. Tai loved the drama, and I was sure the photos would probably be better for it.

After an hour and a half of plastering on smiles, I went upstairs to the writing office. I avoided the set because I didn't want to face the truth. Since I couldn't effect change there without throwing a huge fit, I decided to passive-aggressively chastise Tamika for her lackluster writing.

But even that was disappointing, because Tamika claimed she had only barely sketched out the scenes before Frieda Weiner grabbed them and then rewrote them on the network's behalf. Frankly, this worried me even more, because it meant the network was quietly usurping *everyone's* duties, not just mine. Richard's role (and allegiance) was still unclear.

It was six o'clock by now. Usually I sat around until eight or so, catching up on my work, but not today—it was time to get out of here. I could do my work at home, even if it meant busting open that packet of school homework and seeing what fresh Leo Tolstoy hell awaited me.

I wandered past the stage on my way to the parking lot and decided to poke my head in. In one corner of the massive hangar that was our soundstage were all the indoor sets—like Marco's cabin and the French brasserie where Sarah worked. They were all queerly shallow, but with lighting and camera tricks, they would look much bigger.

The biggest set we had built was of the bridge that spans the literal Deception Pass—the rocky gorge with its black-sand riverbanks and evergreens. Of course, our tree-covered mountains were merely a backdrop and the evergreens in our forest all had their tops missing. Keith had nicknamed this set "the Bridge Over Troubled Water" when I'd shown him the sketches. It wasn't that clever, but I'd laughed like it was.

"That's a wrap for Jacqueline," bellowed the AD.

Francesca walked off the bridge and toward me while the crew quickly prepared to film another setup.

"How's our creator?" she asked me with a toothy Crest-Whitestripped smile.

"Cuttin' out early today," I said. "I'm exhausted."

"Need a ride?" she offered. "Your mom still has a few scenes left."

The way she said it, I felt like a fourth grader waiting for her mommy to pick her up from school.

"Um, sure, thanks."

"Super. Just give me two minutes and I'll be ready to go."

Fifteen minutes later, we climbed into Francesca's Prius and drove off the lot, heading toward the smoggy orange and purple sunset. It wasn't long before we ran out of chitchat about the upcoming Barneys sale and whether or not Ryan Seacrest was hot or just sort of cute.

After a silence that lasted through three lights while we waited to make a left onto Santa Monica Boulevard, Francesca said, "Look, can I make a suggestion?"

Uh-oh, I thought. I'd *known* there was something motivating her act of chauffeur kindness.

"Of course," I replied.

"Dallas told me about the showdown with Richard. He's upset."

"I don't blame him. I am, too."

"I think we need to do something."

We? Hmmm. What precisely did *we* need to do? I didn't like being treated as a co-conspirator. But instead of saying this, I said, "About what?"

"Dallas is the core of this show. He's what's going to get people tuning in."

"That's not true—it's an ensemble."

"Right. Look, Mallory, you don't have to sugarcoat it for me. I can objectively see my place in the hierarchy. There's Dallas, then Alexis, then Javier and me, and then the Professor and Mary Ann. But my point is this: Dallas is at his best when he's happy. You should have seen the half-assed performance he was delivering during today's reshoots. Phoning it in would have been an improvement. He was texting it in from God knows where. And if he feels trapped, it's only going to get worse. We need Dallas to be at his best if we have any prayer of making this show a hit. Don't you think?"

Yes, I did think. In particular, I was thinking that it was

clear that Dallas hadn't told Francesca about the talk we'd had. She didn't know that I knew about Shakespeare in the Park. She thought she was my only source of Dallas news. But I wasn't about to admit this.

"What do you suggest we do?" I asked.

"I think that one of the reasons he wants off the show is that he misses his life back in New York. He doesn't really have any friends out here besides me. So I thought maybe we could all go out for dinner tomorrow. Dallas, you, me, and your boyfriend—what's his name? Heath?"

This smelled like a trap to me. Why bring Keith into it?

And then I thought, *why* not *bring Keith into it?* It would probably be good for Dallas to see that I had a boyfriend, and for me to see Dallas seeing that I had a boyfriend, and for Keith to see that even though I spent the day with beautiful actors, he was still the one I came back to.

"You think it would help?" I asked Francesca, without specifying *who* it would help.

"I really do," Francesca said, also not specifying.

"Okay."

"So it's a date? Yay!" Then she kissed her hand and touched it to the roof as we sped through a yellow light.

I've learned from my many years watching soaps that spontaneity is one of the most surefire ways to ruin a relationship (despite what dating columnists might preach). Every time a guy cuts out of work early and decides to bring his honey some flowers and a bottle of wine, she is inevitably either in bed with another man or burying a body in her azalea garden. But I threw caution to the wind and had Francesca drop me at

Keith's. I didn't even know if he was home, but I was pretty sure he wouldn't be in bed with another girl. And if he was burying a body, I hoped it was Frieda Weiner's. Or my mother's. Or Amelia's. Heck, if it was Amelia's, I'd help dig the grave.

Keith lived with his mom and two younger sisters in Culver City. I walked across the crabgrass-filled lawn to his doorway. A sad strand of Christmas lights was still strung above the porch, collecting cobwebs. Usually their bungalow was charming and pretty well maintained, but Keith hadn't had much time to help with the upkeep since he'd upped his hours at CPK.

Keith's mom answered the door with the cordless phone pressed against her ear. She was yelling at the contractor, who was adding a bathroom. Their one-bathroom bungalow was shrinking by the second with Vicki and Connie about to turn thirteen and ten, respectively. A new bathroom was his mom's only option in preventing daily nuclear meltdowns at 7:30 a.m., when everyone was already ten minutes late.

With her hair pulled back into a quick ponytail, her tan complexion, and her kickin' figure, Keith's mom looked more like a girl in search of the perfect wave than a harried mother of three who worked as a nurse (and occasional backup singer). She mouthed "hello" and waved me inside, pointing toward Keith's room while she harangued the contractor for having shown up three hours late and with the wrong sink.

I made my way through the living room and saw Connie sprawled out across the floor with her hand in a box of organic cereal and watching some sort of beach party on MTV. She waved her foot at me as I passed by.

"Happy almost birthday," I said.

"Thanks," she said without much interest.

"Pretty soon, you'll be in the double digits. Ten's a big one."

Connie shrugged, but then turned to me. A serious look settled on her face as she swept a bit of her long, dark hair out of her eye, and she asked, "Do you ever think that maybe you're missing out on the best part of your life? Like, sometimes I think that maybe I didn't really *appreciate* second grade. And now here I am staring down ten like it's a loaded gun and I'm thinking that I should have spent more time riding ponies."

"There will be plenty more time for ponies," I said reassuringly.

She furrowed her brow. "Eh. I never cared much for horses, anyway. They just smell and poo everywhere."

I guessed this girl wasn't a My Little Pony fan.

"He's back there, by the way," she said, gesturing to the backyard.

She returned her attention to the television and the problems of being nine going on ten. I made my way through the screen door and crossed the concrete patio toward the little structure that was once a one-car garage, then was Keith's father's recording studio, and now was Keith's bedroom.

Keith's dad had been one of innumerable rockers who prowled The Rainbow and sired kids with more than one girlfriend. Roxanne, Keith's mom, had been the only one he'd married, but it ended shortly after Connie's birth. Last I heard, he was holed up in Oregon somewhere with a new girlfriend and a new baby. The child support checks came about as frequently as winning lottery tickets.

Keith was sitting at his desk in boxers and a T-shirt that had seen better days. He was bent over a textbook, distractedly chewing on his thumbnail. I knocked at the door and he turned around, revealing the super-cute reading glasses that he never let me see him wear.

"Look who it is, Puddles," he said to the fluffy gray cat curled in his lap. He lifted her off and got up to kiss me.

Puddles darted through my calves as Keith brushed his lips across mine and whispered a hello. His breath smelled of crunchy peanut butter. Strangely, it was kind of sexy. I hoped my own wild cherry lip gloss tasted like jelly.

"Yum," he said, pulling back and smacking his lips. "Tasty."

He took off his glasses, mussed his hair with an eye on his reflection in the window, and asked, "What brings you to my neck of the woods, Little Red Riding Hood?"

"I was on my way to Grandma's, but I just felt spontaneous and decided instead to come see my wolf," I said.

Keith growled a long *Grrrrrrrr* and pawed at me. I shrieked and giggled.

"Looks like you got a haircut," he said.

In all the hoopla, I'd totally forgotten. I reflexively touched my head just to confirm that my hair was indeed short now.

"What do you think? Do you like it?"

"Does this answer your question?"

He pulled me down onto the bed and we rolled around while he told me in kisses just how much he liked my new 'do. *Mental note: Get your hair cut more often.*

After we passed some time confirming how much we liked each other's hair, I started telling him about my day. About half an hour into my detailed play-by-play of the photo shoot debacle with Richard and Dallas, I noticed that Keith was dozing off. I suppose my one-woman Japanese Noh play about an afternoon in the life of me was not as captivating as I'd hoped.

"Am I boring you?" I asked, pretty sure of the answer.

Keith stifled a yawn. "No, not at all, babe."

I cocked my eyebrow to indicate *Yeah, right.* But I appreciated the lie nonetheless.

I realized I hadn't really bothered to ask Keith about his day. In fact, I hadn't asked him anything at all beyond whether he liked my hair.

"I'm sorry, I haven't found out what's new with you. What did you get up to today?" I asked.

"Uh . . . school . . . then work . . . then home . . . then home-work. Ba-da-bing, ba-da-boom!" He mimed shooting himself in the head.

"Fascinating. A real page-turner," I said.

"I save the drama for you."

"Here's another question. . . ."

"Goody. I hope it involves math," Keith said.

"What are you doing tomorrow night?"

"Are you suggesting that we finally follow through on our blood oath to bring anarchy and revolution to the streets of America?" he asked dryly.

"I was hoping to save that 'til the weekend," I responded.

"Oh, well. In that case I have to work."

"Really?" I wasn't sure if he was still joking.

"Yep—five 'til closing. It's AWESOME!"

It sucked that Keith had to work so much. Most of the kids we went to school with didn't need after-school jobs just to guarantee a couple of twenties in their wallet come the weekend, but with an absentee father, Keith was not as fortunate. It's not like his mom didn't make a respectable living, because she did, but with three kids and a Southern California mortgage, she couldn't really treat Keith to all the fast food and gas a teenage boy needs.

"I don't suppose you could get someone to cover. . . ."

"You have something planned?"

I proceeded to explain the dilemma with Dallas and how Francesca thought dinner would be a good idea and that when she'd suggested a double date, I just for some reason said sure.

Keith sighed and walked to the window, which was caked with the remnants of a thousand sprinkler cycles.

"Yeah, I guess I could get Jimmy to take my shift. It's just that I kind of need all the shifts I can get if I want to afford that snowboard trip up to Mammoth later this month."

"Well, if it's money you're worried about," I said, "I can totally pay you for your time. Dinner will be on me."

Suddenly all the air seemed to get sucked out of the room as Keith turned red. "I am *not* a charity case, Mallory," he said.

"I didn't mean it like that," I mumbled.

He took a deep breath. "I know you didn't mean anything by it." He paused. "So let's just drop this subject right now. You never need to pay me to go out with you."

"Keith, I know that," I tried to explain. "You are not Julia Roberts to my Richard Gere. I just thought that since this was, like, totally a favor, the least I could do was buy you a burrito. Consider yourself my freelance consultant."

"A what?" he asked.

"Oh, one of those titles like 'associate producer' that are just vague enough to cover anything," I said.

He sat down next to me on the bed. His cheeks were still flushed, but I could see he wasn't as upset.

"Well, as fun as it sounds to be your freelance consultant, I'm more than happy to settle for the title of 'boyfriend.' And, as said boyfriend, I will do things like rearrange my *whole frickin' life* just to go to a business dinner with said girlfriend."

I was nervous, but he eased it with a smile.

"And just for the record, the Bank of Keith doesn't accept your personal checks. It only accepts really good, hot, serious, make-your-mother-blush-style kisses."

For good measure, I made a big deposit.

"But what about the School of Life, Mallory?
What about the School of Life?"

t h i r t e e n

On the way to work the next morning, my mother hit me up for a bigger part.

"Now that there are going to be more consenting adults on the show, don't you think Vienna deserves some romance of her own?" she asked/told me.

"Mom, you're the guidance counselor."

"Yes, but even guidance counselors have provocative sexual desires!"

They couldn't have sent a limo that stretched long enough for me to get away from this conversation. It was bad enough that her character was named Vienna—an homage to her *Good As Gold* character, Geneva. It had been Mom's idea (she did not use the word *homage*) and the network had loved it. Actually, she wanted her character to be named Paris. I counter-offered Leningrad. We compromised on Vienna.

"Mom," I said now, "nobody wants to know about the guidance counselor's needs and desires. All they want is for the guidance counselor to get them into a good school."

"But what about the School of Life, Mallory? *What about the School of Life?*"

I just looked out the window at the Yum Yum Donuts, knowing if I fell into silence, she would feel she'd made her point.

When I got to the writers' room, Tamika looked like she wanted to use her head to jackhammer the ceiling.

"I think the network's notes are longer than the script!" she groaned.

"Hand 'em over," I said.

Sure enough, the network had gone through every word with a fine-toothed bludgeon. They wanted more sex. They wanted more murder. They wanted more shirts to come off the guys and more bathing suits to go on the girls.

Each change was initialed *FW*.

I looked up at Tamika.

"Who in God's creation is this Frieda Weiner witch, and where does she get off saying what people our age want to watch?" I said, indignant. "I'll bet the last time she went on a date was when soaps were in black-and-white and sponsored by actual detergent companies! I'll give *her* a little *consultation,* if you know what I mean. . . ."

Tamika had gone pale white. Which was pretty impressive, since she's black.

The look in her eyes was unmistakable.

"Frieda Weiner is standing right behind me, isn't she?" I asked.

Tamika nodded.

"Within earshot?"

"Yes," Frieda Weiner's voice said. "Within earshot."

I turned around and faced her. She was shorter than me but had plenty of jewelry to compensate.

"For your information," she said, "I speak on behalf of Webster Strong and all of the network VPs. And, also for your information, my husband and I have been very happily married for the past thirty years. So I don't need to go on *dates.*"

She shoved a few more pages in my general direction.

"More notes," she said.

"We'll take them under consideration," I replied icily.

"You'd better," she replied, then stormed off.

When she was gone, I turned back to Tamika.

"She would never talk like that to me if I were her age, would she?" I asked.

"Probably worse, Lucy Ricardo," Tamika said. "Now let's see the damage she's done this time. . . ."

After a couple of hours of undoing Frieda Weiner's witchwork in the writers' room and a couple of hours of worthless tutoring from Miss Julie, I made my way across the network lot to Trip Carver's office.

Greg looked happy to see me.

"Hey!" he said, getting up from his perch outside Trip's sanctum. "How's it going?"

"Good. Sort of. How are you?"

"Invisibly chained to this desk. But otherwise okay."

"Is Trip back from his—" I stopped myself.

Greg smiled. "Go ahead. Say it."

"No, it's silly."

"Everybody does it."

"Fine. Is Trip back from his trip?"

Greg shook his head. "On the morrow. But he's been talking to Richard about your show."

I raised an eyebrow. I found myself doing this more and more lately.

"Really?"

"Looks like you're going to reshoot the opening credits this weekend. Prepare for a late-night flight on Friday."

This was music to my ears. I leaned over with an invisible scissors and pretended to cut Greg's invisible chain. "Maybe we can get you to come, too," I said.

Greg grinned this boyish, dopey grin that definitely didn't go with the generic-brand suit he was wearing.

"That would be cool," he said.

"We'll see what we can do."

I might have stayed there longer, just to chat, but the phone started ringing again and Greg's chain pulled him back in.

"See you later," he mouthed to me.

"See you in Washington State," I mouthed back.

I headed to the set and found my mother shooting a scene with Alexis. Since they only had one scene together so far, I knew which one it was. Sarah, still heartbroken from having to leave Ryan, is trying to hide her pain from everyone, including Vienna . . . but Vienna sees right through her.

VIENNA
What's wrong, Sarah?

130

                    SARAH
                It's nothing.

                    VIENNA
            No, as much as you try to
        disguise it as nothing, I can
            tell it's something . . .
            something very wrong. You
        might not believe it, Sarah,
        but I know what wrong feels
            like. It doesn't let go.

Only, this was how my mother said it now.

                    VIENNA
            No, you cannot tell me it's
            nothing! It's something,
        Sarah! It's something! You
        have no idea what pain lies
            in my past, what kind of
        wrongs have been infected. No
        matter how hard I try, they
                won't let go!

I knew Richard was in the control booth, and that I should
not be saying a word while I was on the set. But I couldn't help
it. At the very least, we had to get her to say *inflicted* instead of
infected. I was about to yell "STOP!" when my mother surprised me by doing it herself.

"STOP!" she cried. "We must have the lighting fixed this *instant.*"

"What is it, my dear?" Richard's voice asked over the loud-speaker. "Your lighting is perfect. Completely set according to your contractual specifications for interiors."

"I know! But look at the lighting on this poor girl. She looks older than me! I insist that you make it gentler."

Alexis looked at my mother in wonder.

"I had no idea," she said.

My mother patted her on the knee. "Now, don't you worry. I will make sure they give you the best lighting possible. When you've been in The Biz as long as I have, you learn all the tricks."

"Thank you," Alexis said.

"Oh, it's my pleasure," Mom replied.

It was one heck of a performance. I was actually starting to believe that Mom cared about someone besides herself.

They replayed the scene on the monitors, and I saw my mother was absolutely right—the lighting on Alexis needed to be changed. Nobody else had caught it. And Mom knew it without even seeing the footage.

I walked over as Gina fixed Mom's makeup.

"Any chance I could get you to stick to the script?" I asked my mother.

"Oh, I did!" she said breezily. She gestured for Gina to hand over the pages. "I just made a few tweaks."

In other words, she'd scribbled all over the script and made her own dialogue.

"Frieda approved them," Mom added.

I was about to tear out all my hair, and then some of hers.

"I liked the new dialogue," Alexis chimed in. "But you probably meant to say *inflicted* instead of *infected*."

"Thank you!" Mom cried, as if she'd just been given gold. "I'm glad *someone* has an eye on my dialogue besides me. You're such a sweetheart . . . and such a *good* actress."

Alexis actually blushed.

"All right!" the director called. "If you're not one of the actresses, off the set!"

Gina and I stepped to the side . . . and watched as Mom and Alexis completely nailed the take. Alexis's gradual revealing of her pain even moved me . . . and I'd written it. There's nothing quite so silly as crying at your own writing—but if even I could fall for it, I guess it couldn't be that bad.

During the scene, Alexis moved from denial to complete misery. And the minute the director called cut, she popped right into exhilaration—the exhilaration, I knew, of getting the job done right.

"How was it?" she came over and asked me.

"Do I have to say it? You were *fantastic*."

"Yay!" she said, and she—I swear—jumped up and down. "Your mother is *the greatest*. I wouldn't have been able to do it without her. We practiced—I mean, rehearsed—before. And the lighting!"

There was no way to tell her that my mother's kindness was no doubt self-interested. I mean, if Alexis was good in the scene, it would make the scene (and therefore my mother) look good.

Alexis must have sensed that my mind had fallen from yayness.

"What's wrong?" she asked. And then she whispered low, "Is it Dallas?"

That made me stop and pay attention. Did she think I was auditioning to be his Juliet, too?

"What about Dallas?" I asked cautiously.

"Have you seen what we shot this morning?"

I shook my head.

"Well, Dallas wasn't really into it, if you know what I mean. Richard kept yelling at him, and that would only make it worse. Can I be honest?"

"Of course."

"It was kind of like acting with a statue. It's like he's lost his spark. We have to help him get his spark back!"

"Maybe he was just having a bad day," I offered lamely.

"Maybe," Alexis said, but I could tell she didn't believe it. She looked like she was going to cry.

I looked at the corner of the set . . . and saw my mother and Frieda Weiner.

Heading to lunch.

Together.

Now it was me who wanted to cry.

Richard was in his office, eating sushi again.

"Do you get the same thing for lunch every day?" I asked.

He looked at me like my IQ was the same as my age.

"Of course," he said. "Do you know how much time people waste figuring out what to eat? If you add up all the minutes, it's something like three months out of their total lives, assuming they live to sixty. It's insane. Does it really matter what you eat? Is it really worth that much time deciding? If you get it wrong, you can change it next meal. Just don't spend all your life deciding which sandwich you want. There are way more important things to do."

"I just thought you liked sushi," I said.

"No more or less than anything else."

"About Frieda Weiner . . . ," I began.

Richard held up his hand.

"I know, I know. She's interfering. She's got all the drama sense of a mad cow. You want her gone. I know. But Trip and Webster have sent her, so we have to hear her out, then pick our battles. You've got to play their game, Mallory. Because they own the field."

"I think my mother's up to something."

"This is news? Your mother is *always* up to something. That's why I love her. We could all take lessons from your mom on playing the game."

This was not what I wanted to hear. Sensing this, Richard added, "Which isn't to say it's her show. Or Frieda Weiner's show. It's our show. And we'll do what we can to keep it that way."

I didn't like the *our* . . . but it was better than a *their*.

Later that day, a new batch of "notes" came from the network.

Included was this new line:

```
              VIENNA
   Jacqueline, I don't want you
      to think of me as just a
   guidance counselor. I'm not
```

```
          only here to get you into a
        good school. I'm here to help
         you in the School of Life.
```

This, I decided, was a declaration of war.

Don't let her fool you, I reminded myself. *She's out to get you.*

f o u r t e e n

Keith was right on time to pick me up for our "double date" with Francesca and Dallas. He was nervous—a fact that was clear because he was overcompensating to look like he wasn't nervous. As I walked over, Keith got out of the car and opened my door for me. It wasn't even something he thought about, some ploy to impress. It just came naturally.

"How are you, Marilyn?" he said, pulling me into a kiss.

"Out of the park, DiMaggio," I said once we'd stopped. I could feel the nervousness in his kiss. "This'll be fun, I promise. You have nothing to worry about."

"Who said I had anything to worry about?"

Somewhere on Franklin, around the Bourgeois Pig coffeehouse, I broke the bad news.

"So, um, I have to tell you something."

"Uh-oh. That doesn't sound like an intro to 'I just won the lottery. Let's ditch this one-horse town and move to Rio.'"

I looked out the window to see the Scientology Celebrity Centre. I tried to draw strength from the imagined presence of an E-Metering Tom Cruise beyond the wall.

"You know how much of a disaster the opening credits are?"
He nodded.

"Well, we're going to do some additional filming this weekend to fix the opening credits. And we're filming on location in Washington State. And I have to be there."

Keith looked away from the road and repeated, "*This* weekend? Valentine's Day?"

"Unfortunately. But I insisted that I get to stay in town for the dance. The cast is flying up Friday evening, but I said I had to go to the dance first."

"So you're going up Saturday?" he asked.

"Well . . . ," I hemmed, then hawed, "actually, I'm taking the red-eye out of LAX late Friday night."

"So after the dance I get to drive you to the airport? I thought we were going to, well, make some mischief afterward."

"I'll give you a rain check on the mischief."

"What am I supposed to say?" Keith seemed genuinely confused. "I mean, if I tell you I'm not disappointed, it sounds like I don't really care about being with you. And if I say I am disappointed, I sound like a jerk."

"You can say you understand," I said quietly, touching his leg. "You know how crazy things are for me. It'll all calm down after the first episode is completely done. I promise."

Keith sighed and downshifted as we approached the restaurant. Miraculously, he found a parking space.

"Hey?" I asked. "Do you forgive me? I had no choice."

It was sad, the way Keith tried to smile but couldn't do it all the way. "I forgive you," he said. "But at some point I want my girlfriend back."

Cha Cha Cha is an East Side restaurant that's Latin in concept and Brazilian in detail. Located in Silverlake, east of the Highland Curtain, the place is a magnet for alterna-chicks and slim-suited architects. Francesca had picked this place presumably because she lived in nearby Echo Park. But I'm sure its coolness factored in.

I scanned the crowd on the outdoor patio and saw Francesca and Dallas at a table in the back. She waved to get my attention and stood up as we approached, with Dallas following a few beats behind.

He did not look happy.

"Hope you weren't waiting long," I said as I air-kissed Francesca across the table. She extended her hand to Keith.

"Hi, I'm Francesca and this is Dallas. You must be Keith."

"Good guesser, this one," said Keith.

"I knew Mallory had good taste, since she hired me and Dallas. But now it's definitely confirmed." Francesca didn't sound like Francesca at all; instead she sounded like she was auditioning for a sitcom. "Sit. Sit. I ordered a pitcher of sangria and a bottle of Pellegrino. I didn't know if you guys drank or not."

Dallas, I noticed, was sipping a margarita on the rocks. The salt stuck to the top of his lip, and I tried not to have any visible feelings about doing something about it. None of us was twenty-one, but Francesca's aura of celebrity was sure to get us served. I, personally, wasn't about to start drinking with my cast. Because my mother was such a boozehound, I usually saved the sips for special occasions. I remembered the time I had felt compelled to sample her "grown-up lemonade" when

I was about nine. I spent the rest of that afternoon worshipping the porcelain goddess. Keith, I noticed, had quickly poured himself a glass of the sangria.

"Don't forget you're driving," I whispered.

"Just one glass," he said through the side of his mouth.

"I'm really excited we could get together and do this," said Francesca, taking control of the table.

Keith raised his glass. "Let's have a toast—to my beautiful girlfriend, and to her talented cast. Live long and prosper."

"Hear! Hear!" chirped Francesca as we clinked glasses. Dallas barely lifted his.

The conversation turned to traffic and other polite, uninteresting things. Three of us chatted. One of us didn't.

"You're awful quiet, Dallas," I said.

I kept catching him looking at Keith. He wouldn't look at me.

"Long day," he said sullenly.

"Well," I said, "I've been working hard on making those rewritten scenes work. It's not like the whole murder mystery is going to be alchemized into gold or anything, but I think we at least pressed it into a semi-precious gemstone. I'm thinking of making my mom the killer."

"But I wanted to be the killer!" Francesca exclaimed.

I was shocked. "Really?"

"Kidding, honey. Kidding. I know I'm playing the bad girl, but if you start me at murder, I'll have nowhere to go. I don't want to be poisoning the Deception Pass water supply by week six."

Francesca said something to Keith and he laughed. Was he enjoying himself? Strange.

Dinner did not progress easily.

At one point, Keith excused himself to go to the "little boys' room." Then Francesca's phone rang.

"It's Alexis," she said, then headed to a quieter spot to take the call.

Leaving me and Dallas. Alone. Together.

"He's very nice," Dallas said.

"I know," I said, irritated.

"A shame," he mumbled.

"What?"

He looked down at the table, then back up at me. He started to lean in and say something, but was interrupted by the waiter delivering his next drink. "Mallory . . ."

He stopped.

"What is it, Dallas?"

He shook his head. I leaned in, but he leaned away.

"It's nothing. Don't worry about it." He looked over my shoulder. "Francesca thinks this will cheer me up. But it only makes me miss home more, you know?"

It was now clear what Dallas was looking at—Francesca, coming back from her call. She was like a circuit breaker to whatever had just connected the two of us.

He took another gulp of his drink. The salt sat on his lip in that way again. I had to fight the urge to lick it off myself.

Fortunately, she sat back down before I could give in.

"*She's* on her way over," she said. "There was no avoiding it. She heard me and Dallas talking about it earlier, and *someone*"—she glared at Dallas—"invited her along."

"What?" Dallas asked. "Is she not allowed to be seen with us?"

I had to agree with him. But clearly there was some Francesca/Alexis issue I didn't know about.

"I thought you two were friends," I said.

"My publicist would say that we are great friends," Francesca replied. "But that doesn't mean I trust her."

Which was funny to hear her say, since it was pretty much how I felt about Francesca, at least before seeing her in action tonight.

The tension between Alexis and Francesca became clearer once Alexis arrived. Keith was back from the bathroom by then, and Alexis pulled a chair up to our table, placing herself smack-dab in the middle of the two boys.

"Ooh, what's this?" she asked Dallas. Then she took a swig before he could respond. "Yummers."

"Come here often, Alexis?" Francesca asked coolly.

"Oh, sure. I totally love Mexican food."

"Then you should go to El Cid. This place serves Brazilian."

Alexis giggled. "Whatev." She signaled to the waiter and pointed to the margarita. "I'll have one of these."

Uh-oh, I thought. *Who let the teen actress away from her domineering stage mother?*

"How'd you get here?" I asked. She was fifteen. There was no way she had a license.

"I cabbed it. Mom has a meeting of CAMERA—you know, Child Actors' Mothers Earning the Right Amount. They get together to bitch and moan about how evil everyone in Hollywood is. I'm supposed to be at home, learning my lines. One of you can give me a ride back, right?"

"Sure," Keith said, ever the good sport.

"You're so *great*," Alexis said, putting her hand on his arm. "Who are you?"

"Mallory's boyfriend."

"Oh." Alexis took her hand away . . . and moved her other hand onto Dallas's arm. "How are you doing, Dallas?" she asked earnestly.

I don't want to see you this way, I thought.

Francesca had a side conversation with the waiter, and Alexis was never served her own drink. She didn't seem to notice. She seemed drunk on the company instead. The male company, that is.

Talk turned to all the failed pilots Francesca, Alexis, and Dallas had been in—mostly Alexis, who was a California girl through and through. Though I'd been raised around cameras, she was raised *on* camera. Her first TV appearance was as a diapered baby in a Gerber commercial. Then came the pilots: *Sweet Nothings* (kids! running a candy shop!), *Desperate Schoolgirls* (girls! getting caught by the mean headmistress!), and *Tweenville* (for the Sci Fi channel! about tweens who take over a town after adults mysteriously disappear!). I sensed Alexis had told the story of each failure a million times before, but I had to admit it was still entertaining. Despite her lack of a breakout hit, she had worked constantly and had the cloying air of seen-it-all naiveté that is prevalent among child actors. The amazing thing was that it didn't come across at all when she was playing Sarah.

While Alexis was telling us all about how she'd blown her audition for the *Law & Order: Child Services* spin-off, Keith leaned over to me and said, "You having fun, Holmes?"

"My publicist would say, 'Yeah,' Watson. You?"

"Not bad myself. So these are your new friends, huh?"

I looked at Francesca, Dallas, and Alexis. It hadn't even occurred to me to think of them that way. But I guess they were all I had, now that my high school friendships had flamed out.

"I guess so," I said. But even as I said it, it didn't feel entirely true. It was more complicated than just friendship.

I reached for Keith's hand under the table, and he took it.

"I'm glad you're here," I said.

And I really was. Until I saw Dallas looking at our arms going under the table.

I tried to catch his glance. But he'd already turned away.

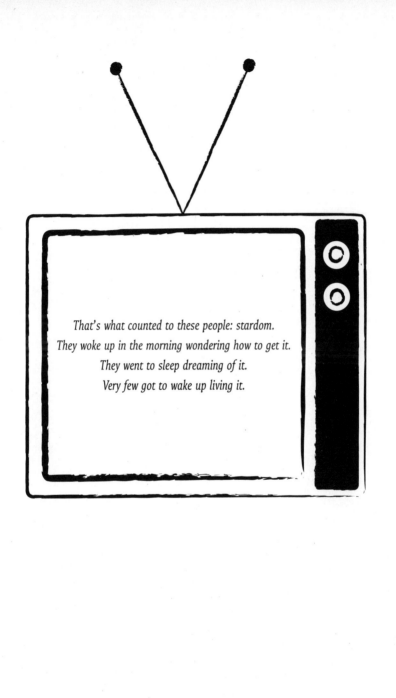

That's what counted to these people: stardom.
They woke up in the morning wondering how to get it.
They went to sleep dreaming of it.
Very few got to wake up living it.

fifteen

Dallas continued to phone his performance in for the rest of the week. Even the crew, who usually ignored anything not related to their union-sanctioned duties, were beginning to notice his lack of enthusiasm. One simple shot of him answering his phone took thirty-seven takes—an eternity when most shots get two or three takes, max.

The only saving grace was that we were shutting down production early on Friday so that the cast could attend my mother's *Good As Gold* Farewell Party. Naturally, I was expected to attend as well. But my thoughts were more focused on the Valentine's Dance that night, and my quick departure after. In the interest of spending as much time with Keith as possible before I dashed, I'd invited him to the party, too, but he said he couldn't miss a chemistry test. Scooter, however, had taken the day off school to attend. I was upstairs taking a catnap in my bedroom when my mother burst through the door with a crazed look in her eye.

"Mallory! Wake up! It's a disaster."

"What?" I asked groggily.

"The chocolate fountain exploded and ruined my dress."

Indeed it had. My mother's white organza gown looked like a black-and-white cookie.

"What do you want me to do about it? I'm not a dry cleaner."

"That's not what I meant, Little Miss Snotface. I need you to go downstairs and oversee the caterers while I find *something, anything* else to wear."

I wasn't too worried about my mother's problem. Her closet was stocked with more designer ready-to-wear than all the tents in Bryant Park combined. I was confident she would find a new ensemble in no time, equally as gaudy as the one she recently ruined.

"Don't you have a party coordinator?"

"Of course I do, but I don't trust her. Carly seems a little flighty."

If my own airborne mother considered this woman flighty, she had to be a born-again Amelia Earhart.

I pushed myself off the bed with a burst of that helpful can-do attitude that usually results in a serious backfire. I was going to head downstairs, but my mother stopped me with a "You think you're wearing *that*?"

That was jeans and a flowy top—the kind that the children of the children of the sixties liked to wear. I was pretty sure my mother had bought it for my last birthday. Or one of her assistants had. It undoubtedly came from Fred Segal (upstairs, not downstairs).

"It's a garden party, Mom. This is supposed to be casual."

"Does this Vera Wang look casual?"

"No, it looks like crap-ture now."

She almost slapped me. I backed away out of instinct and decided not to press it.

"I'll put on a sundress," I conceded.

"And heels," she commanded.

"I repeat, it's a *garden party*—I'm not trudging around our muddy grass in heels. You get a dress, but I get flats."

"Fine. But do it fast because I'm afraid that chocolate fountain is going to flood the dance tent."

That sounded like biblical retribution to me. But I kept my mouth shut. My mother was ready to pounce on any insubordination and I was not about to give her more ammunition.

Downstairs, in the yard where the tent had been erected, Scooter had already made himself at home. He was wearing a dandy suit and a *Good As Gold* souvenir tie that you can buy on the network's Web site.

"Scooter! I'm so glad to see you." It was nice to have a friendly face in my home for once. "Stay by my side at all times. I don't want to be left alone with any of these people."

"These people," he said in all seriousness, "are not people. They are stars of Daytime. I'd love to be left alone with any of them."

"Sure, Scoot, but it's not your show that cost them their jobs." I'd managed to save a lot of the people from *Good As Gold*—like Gina—and add them to the staff of *Likely Story*, but not everyone had been able to switch ships.

"Point taken. I'll be your wingman at all times."

"You're positively a dream," I said. Because I knew he'd like to hear it that way.

The party itself was so over the top that I wouldn't be surprised if it could have been seen from space. The chocolate fountain was the least of the expensive horrors my mother had concocted. The Handwriting Analyst. The Juggler. The Caribbean Steel Drum Band playing Paul Simon songs.

At first I felt fortunate to have Scooter glued to my side as the guests began arriving in their Beemers (those who had worked on *Good As Gold* for five years or more) and their Hondas (those whose characters had suffered mysterious and abrupt deaths off boats or planes when a younger, more attractive female character had been introduced to seduce, marry, and betray one of the male leads). After sixteen years of watching these day players come and go, I'd forgotten who many of them were. Desperate to approximate intimacy with me (a new possible employer), they all gushed like oil wells during a boom time. I would have had no idea who some were had Scooter not been there to identify each and every one. He even provided the perfect comments, saying things like "Laura Brock, you were absolutely devastating in that scene when they told you that you'd been exposed to bird flu," or "It's so neat to meet you, Mr. Strich—your marriage to Muffi Mattison was second only to Luke and Laura's."

The guests beamed at the comments. It made them feel like real stars again. Were they ever real stars? In Hollywood it goes from Movies to TV to Music in terms of Celebrity Importance. There are exceptions that prove the rule, of course, but soap stars are somewhere around that guy who was once on that arc of *Law & Order* and Oprah's latest celebrity dietician.

After about half an hour of conversations I wouldn't remember under penalty of death, my mother reappeared. Like any lesser goddess, she made her presence known with everything short of medieval trumpet players. She sashayed down our backyard patio staircase (my mom LOVES a good staircase—I think it dates to her days watching *Gone with the Wind* as a girl) into the party, showing off her new gown. A Balenciaga, I think.

Everyone fawned over her like she was the Queen of England. Or, rather, the Queen of Daytime . . . recently deposed. Yes, she was on *my* show, but she wasn't the STAR. And that's what counted to these people: stardom. They woke up in the morning wondering how to get it. They went to sleep dreaming of it. Very few got to wake up living it.

Scooter continued to stay glued to my arm when my own cast started showing up. In all of the madness of party preparation, I hadn't really thought obsessively about the fact that was striking me now: *Dallas was about to see my house.* It's not like there was anything embarrassing around—my mother was *not* the type to hang up third-grade studio portraits or blue ribbons from pony camp. But, when it came down to it, I was a little embarrassed by the lack of embarrassing things. Until you got to my bedroom, you wouldn't even know I lived in the house.

Dallas and Francesca were in nearly matching garden party outfits—him looking suave in a vest and skinny tie, with flat-front Costume National pants, his white sleeves immaculately rolled up to look like he hadn't bothered; her looking like a low-key flapper, complete with beaded purse. I noticed she had braved heels. Behind them, Alexis looked fresh as a breeze in a floral print, and Javier looked ready to party in South

Beach in a Rag & Bone T-shirt designed to emphasize every contour of his chest. Even Richard looked like he'd worked hard on what to wear, sporting a fancy navy blazer with hairline pinstripes of silver. He'd brought my mother roses, which she accepted with delight.

I sensed Scooter teetering next to me.

"Mallory," he said nervously. "Do you think I could—I mean, would it be okay if I—I mean, I should probably go say hi to your mom, right? Because, you know, she invited me."

"It's okay, wingman. I cut you loose."

I watched as he joined the cluster around my mother, like a member of the Royal Court. I suppose for him it was like being at the Daytime TV version of Buckingham Palace. I envied that a little. Growing up amidst it, more aware of the skeletons in the closet than the gilded wood doors that covered said closets, I was rarely overwhelmed by a Hollywood party. I knew these things got written up a lot in magazines as glamorous "don't-you-wish-you-were-there" affairs. Three photos of anything can make it look good. But with all the tragic facelifts and early nineties gowns dusted off by ladies who once had money but now only had memories of it, *Us Weekly* would be lucky to get one usable shot of the *Good As Gold* last hurrah. Hopefully, it would have Dallas in it. Maybe a little celebrity would give him back the spark we so desperately needed.

Or would it send him fleeing to New York?

Dallas and Francesca were standing in front of the slightly ominous pink bougainvillea bush, which had started out in a small corner of the yard and now nearly encompassed the pool house. The flowers made it look something like a fairy-tale cottage or one of those weird Thomas Kinkade paintings with old mills and candlelit windows you see in malls. Except that inside this sprightly cottage were not kindhearted homespun peasants and their enchanted friends but rather the accumulation of lots of unused pool equipment. Neither my mother nor I swam. Nobody swims in LA. It's like walking.

I realized I had been standing there, in the middle of my backyard, with the blank look of a girl who's seen too much, done too much, and been ignored too much in her short lifetime. It's a stare you'll see at a lot of barbecues in Bel Air during June: the empty eye that comes with being treated by your famous or rich parents like an accessory. That relationship is something that makes you feel like you're competing against a Birkin bag or a canary diamond or the power shuffle at Paramount. The kids almost always lose that competition.

As I headed over to Dallas and Francesca, Dallas raised his can of Pepsi One in my direction in a mock toast. I had only gotten the "hi" out of my mouth when, like all experienced monarchs, my mother took her stage—in this case, our gazebo. The day was just starting to edge into twilight, and she looked glorious. Somehow, my mother could even control natural lighting. Did she have a contract with God?

"Thank you, everyone, for coming," she said grandly. "It has been truly amazing to work with all of you for at least part of the twenty-three years I spent on *Good As Gold*. We had our ups and downs, of course. Fortunately, of the six of us sent to death row, only one of us was actually gassed. Speaking of which, we're *thrilled* to see you here, Asa."

Tepid applause echoed off stucco and stone walls around the garden. Asa waved his hand in the air. My mother was

155

probably upset that the applause had not been for her and that she'd never had the opportunity to be gassed (and, of course, revived . . . although that hadn't been Asa's fate). Her character *had* been found guilty of a capital crime twice . . . but both verdicts had been overturned. One was because the judge was her secret lover (inside the prison! Is that allowed *anywhere?*). The second time she discovered that Ramona, her arch-nemesis and cell mate, had actually been the murderess. (Small world.) But Ramona didn't get "gassed," as my mother so delicately put it, either. I'm not sure what circumstances led to that. It likely involved blackmail or marriage or sex. Probably the combination of all three.

Framed by the lattice of the gazebo, my mother continued:

"I don't want to take up the spotlight, but I think we all know that *Good As Gold*'s untimely end was foolish. And I have a feeling they'll be regretting their decision any week now. No show will ever be as great as ours. Remember that. *Remember.*" She paused with that classic soap pause—the kind where you feel like the actor is marking time until the next commercial break.

"So get back to eating and drinking—we've got gobs and gobs of hors d'oeuvres and champagne. I love you. I truly, truly do."

I had spent over a decade and a half being annoyed, flustered, or angry at my mother. Now I was furious. Not because she hadn't even mentioned *Likely Story*. I understood that— who wants to bring up the show that's replacing a canceled one at the cancelee's party? But the part about no show ever being as great . . . and the fact that the mistake of canceling *Good As Gold* would be evident "any week now"—how could that not be taken as the biggest maternal bitch slap since Medea killed her kids?

That's when I realized: I didn't have to stand here and take this. I could leave.

I went to my room and fumed for a while. That's where Javier and Tamika found me.

"Girl, you get out of that bed," Tamika ordered.

"No," I said.

"Stuff is going on downstairs."

"And I don't want any part of it," I said, burying my face in my ergonomic pillow.

"Let me take it from here," Javier interjected. He sat down on my bed, stroked my hair in that pleasing but completely nonsexual way that only a gay friend can. He took a deep breath. "Okay, there is no proof to confirm this, but I over-heard Alexis conspiring with Richard and your mom."

"Conspiring? What is this? The Bush administration? Alexis is fifteen. She's not capable."

"Now, I admit I had some of the *Good As Gold* punch—which is strong, I'll admit—but I heard her say to your mom that *Likely Story* would be a much bigger hit if . . . well . . . her character was revealed to be Vienna's long-lost daughter!"

"What?" I bolted up. "You must have misheard."

"I hope I did, babe," said Javier. "But you had best be checking that out."

"What did Richard say?"

"He didn't say yes . . . and he didn't say no. Then he started to tell your mom about how he'd obsessed over *Good As Gold* when he was in college. It was a little freaky."

So now Alexis was working her own angle while Dallas

agonized, Richard went gaga over my mom's old role, and the opening credits needed to be reshot and re-edited in a nano-second.

This, I was discovering, was the difference between writing and television:

In writing, it's just you and your words.

In television, there are so many other people who can mess them up.

They say to keep your friends close and your enemies closer. But who could tell the difference at this point?

Desperate times called for desperate measures,
and I thought my mother, in her drunken stupor
of geniality, might offer a way out.

s i x t e e n

The party wound down after my mom showed the gag reel. Gag reels are usually made up of flubs on the set and are traditionally shown at cast parties for fun. But instead of bloopers my mother had assembled a fifteen-minute montage of her greatest hits. My mother's greatest acting talent has always been in reacting. Reacting to bad news. Reacting to scandals exposed. Reacting to the séance in which her great-grandmother came back to life and told her about the family curse that started when her great-great-grandfather had stolen some magic beans.

Most of the other actors were pissed they hadn't been included in the reel. But while all that drama was being screened, I tried to dig around the ambrosia salads and deviled quail eggs to see if there was any more gossip about the new Alexis-Mom-Richard axis. Though my Nancy Drew routine was hardly producing any results beyond what I already knew, and Javier was worth about half a Bobbsey Twin, it was all interrupted by Scooter, who had the most shocking news of all: The Valentine's Dance was less than half an hour away.

The time had indeed slipped away like sands through the hourglass. The sun was setting on Sunset Boulevard and Keith would be here any moment. Since Scooter was already dressed to the nines, he was heading straight over to Bryce McKibbon's house on Doheny to meet up with their friends. He had brought Bryce's boutonniere with him and had left it resting peacefully in the Sub-Zero fridge while everything else continued to wither around me.

I hoped Keith would be the fashionably late type so I might have a little time. I jumped into crisis mode—the zero to sixty in four seconds flat that made me feel like a sixteen-year-old Lambo (as in -*rghini*).

Tamika was heading toward the valets, tossing her scarf behind her like she always did. I raced down the lawn and grabbed her by the arm.

"You can't leave yet," I yelped.

"I've been roasting like a Peruvian potato in this sun for hours, Mal. And I'm meeting some of my USC film friends at the ArcLight in, like, twenty minutes."

"This is an emergency. I have to get dressed for the Valentine's Dance. I totally let the time get away from me and I'm not ready." I took a deep breath and pleaded, "Please. I need girl support."

"You got it, honey. I had a homecoming debacle my sophomore year that took two years of therapy and four prescriptions to get over. I vowed never to let that happen to anyone again. I almost started a foundation."

We started back up the hill to the house.

"How much time do we have?" she asked.

"None." I grabbed a white rose from a nearby table and bit

the stem off with my teeth. This would have to do for a boutonniere.

"Do you have a dress?"

"I meant to borrow one from wardrobe today, but I totally forgot."

That's when God gave me just a little gift. There was Gina, handing out flower arrangements to departing guests. I quickly explained the situation.

Scant seconds later, we had ascended the stairs and were in my room working like a well-oiled machine. Gina was combing out my hair while I was applying the first coat of base to cover my red skin. Tamika was ransacking my closet looking for a dress.

"This closet is a wasteland," she said. "I've seen monks with better color sense than you."

"I have some dresses in there, don't I? What about that black cocktail one?"

"You mean this?" she said, holding up a knee-length charcoal Miss Sixty with ruffled taffeta princess sleeves.

"Yeah." I frowned.

"Maybe if you gave it a dye job and ruffle-ectomy before transporting yourself back in time five years."

"You might have to go back more than five years," mumbled Gina.

"You're not helping," I told them both.

Just as I was thinking I couldn't get any more despondent, my mother waltzed in with a snifter of brandy and a haughty air of self-congratulation wafting from her like Chanel No. 5.

"What's going on in here?"

"Don't worry about it, Mom."

"Don't you think it was a *wonderful* party? Everyone had such a *splendid* time."

"Yes, it was," said Gina. "Everyone was complimenting the canapés. And your dress! Everyone loved your dress."

My mother, it seemed, was a little confused to find Gina out of the dressing room and in my bedroom.

"Why is Gina doing your hair? And who is this black girl rooting through your closet?"

"That's Tamika, Mom. You've met her a bunch of times. She's a writer on the show."

"Oh, Tamika!" she said, as if she actually remembered. "I didn't recognize you with your new hairstyle."

Tamika had not changed her hairstyle in five years, but whatever. I just wanted my mother out of my room.

"I'm running late for my high school dance," I told her. "I know that surely means *nothing* to you. Keith will be here any minute and I don't have anything to wear."

"Why didn't you say so? I just asked what was going on. There's no reason to be as nasty as a divorce lawyer about it."

I suppose this was true if you didn't count the fact that she'd announced to everyone at the party that I would essentially never be as great as her, and that she was probably plotting against me with my producer and female star.

But desperate times called for desperate measures, and I thought my mother, in her drunken stupor of geniality, might offer a way out. So I sucked it up and said, "I'm sorry. It's just that I'm really frazzled."

My mother lolled about on my bed, kicking off her heels to reveal the panty hose beneath. She flexed her toes and mentioned, in an offhanded way, as if she was telling me that soy milk was in the fridge, that she had something that might work.

"Why didn't we think of that?!" Tamika exclaimed with the gusto of a Scrabble enthusiast who'd just found a way to use her ten-point Q for a triple-word score. "Your mom's closet must be chock-full of couture just waiting to be served à flambée at your high school gym."

Tamika, knowing my mother blissfully less well than I, bounded out of the room behind her with glee—hopeful for the classic Tom Ford–era Gucci jersey dress my mother surely had (but I knew would never let me wear).

Then there was a rare moment of silence. Gina was fussing and spritzing, but I felt all the pressures of the day collide in a perfect storm of excitement, dread, anger, exhaustion, and, somewhere, buried deep beneath the rest, hope.

It was overwhelming.

Gina saw this and asked me what was going on. I told her about the attempted coup.

"This isn't Communist Russia," she said consolingly. "No one is planning any coup. Your mother has never seen a pie that she hasn't stuck her finger into. I haven't heard anything, which is unusual if there is in fact something to be heard. But I'll put my ear to the ground and report back."

I pulled myself together just in time for Tamika and my mother to burst back into the room.

"Here it is!" Tamika squealed while my mother polished off the last of her brandy.

And, indeed, there it was. A timeless, midnight-blue silk floor-length dress. Low-cut in the back. Demure but seductive in the front—like a whispered, secret promise.

But would it fit? The Million-Dollar Question. And the answer was a resounding Yes.

As Gina dabbed on the last bits of eyeliner and lipstick, my mother stood back and gushed, "You look like a zillion euros. Or ten zillion yen."

Don't let her fool you, I reminded myself. *She's out to get you.*

The doorbell rang. Prince Charming had arrived, and Cinderella was heading for her ball.

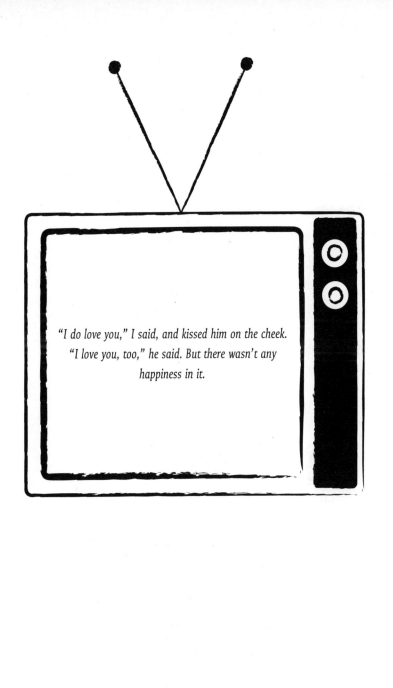

"I do love you," I said, and kissed him on the cheek. "I love you, too," he said. But there wasn't any happiness in it.

s e v e n t e e n

There are four major dances every year at my high school. Prom and homecoming are the most important, with the various coronations and traditions surrounding them. The Snow Ball is probably the least important. The Valentine's Dance is the lone fiery ruby in the midst of a drab desert of February. Its timing on the calendar gets it more attention than it deserves. Kind of like the Golden Globes.

Keith looked amazing in his thrift-store Duckie Brown suit. The French cuffs of his shirt peeked out from the blazer while the cuff links—one of the few things his father had left him—glinted with the reflected glow of the dashboard. Tom Waits crooned softly in the background about the heart of Saturday night.

Gina had snapped the obligatory digital pre-dance pics that will never be downloaded or printed. We made a handsome couple—I was pretty sure of that. I wanted people to tell us what beautiful babies we'd have. (Not that I was looking to test this hypothesis anytime soon.)

When we pulled into the school parking lot, it was already jammed with limos and kids driving their daddies' cars. A Hummer limo was blocking three of the lanes while its passengers disembarked. Behind it was gridlock. Unwilling to wait for the traffic to move or the ice caps to melt, whichever came first, Keith made a fourteen-point turn and took us back out of the parking lot. We found street parking about a block away.

I started to climb out of the car, but Keith stopped me.

"I have something for you," he said.

Oh, no. A Valentine's gift. I knew I'd forgotten yet another thing this week. He was about to give me something wonderful, no doubt, and I had nothing but a flight to the Pacific Northwest to offer in return.

Keith clicked open the glove compartment and revealed a perfect little powder-blue box that I did not need to inspect in order to know that it had *Tiffany & Co.* printed in black letters on the top.

"Oh, Keith, you shouldn't have. . . ." Whatever it was, it must have cost him years of his California Pizza Kitchen salary.

"Wait 'til you open it. You might hate it."

"That's doubtful when it comes in a box from Tiffany's."

"It's not an omelet."

"I was hoping for pancakes."

However, instead of breakfast, the box held the most perfect and lovely silver charm bracelet. It had one charm, a little heart. Keith was good—really good. And what I couldn't tell him was that the effort he must have made to get it for me meant just as much to me as the bracelet itself.

"I love it," I gushed as he undid the clasp and fit it around my wrist.

"I figure we can get some more charms for upcoming big events. Like our anniversary or your big premiere."

I kissed him long and hard, meaning every second of it. Then I stopped and looked away, embarrassed.

"What's wrong?" he asked.

"I feel like a total jerk."

"Why?"

I looked out the window, trying but failing not to stare at the gorgeous bracelet.

"I forgot to get you a present."

"Oh. Well, I wasn't expecting one. Valentine's Day is sort of for girls anyway," he said sympathetically.

"It's just another example of how well you treat me and how distant and detached I've become. I want you to know that I'm trying, I really am, to get my life in order. You belong at the top."

"Hey, hey . . . ," he said, using his thumb to stop the forming tear in my eye before it could ruin Gina's work. "Mallory, I know you're overwhelmed right now. I mean, we're teenagers—we're always overwhelmed unless we're stoned or medicated into oblivion or just plain stupid. So it's only natural that you're having to learn how to balance things. I'm not going anywhere. I'm gonna be here to help you figure it out. You waited for me—now it's my turn."

I smiled weakly. "I love you."

Keith smiled and pecked me on the lips. Then he put his mouth to my ear and softly said, "I love you, too." He pulled away. "Now let's go dance to some bad white-boy rap."

The dance was being held in the school's new Culture and Science Building. How and why these two disciplines came to be married is still a mystery to me. A wonder of poor design, the building has a huge center room that is never used for anything other than the occasional physics club meeting or impromptu drama rehearsal. Tonight it had been draped lazily with crepe paper and balloons that showed a surprising lack of imagination. With so many home design shows popping up all over cable, I assumed the decoration committee would have set a higher standard for itself.

In a surprising bit of eighties variation from the DJ, we entered the room just as he dropped "Somebody to Love" by Queen.

"I love this song," Keith exclaimed, seized by the blaring guitar. He grabbed my hand and pulled me behind him toward the dance floor. No one was on it, but that didn't stop him from gettin' jiggy with his vintage glam rock. I grinned and joined him. I loved that I had a boyfriend who loved Freddie Mercury. Even if everyone was staring at us, judging us silently.

I was trying hard not to feel out of place. Even though I'd escaped, I still wanted to think, if only for tonight, that I belonged at this school.

After the song was over, we ran into Scooter.

He was escorting Bryce through the photo gauntlet.

"Hey, guys," Scooter said gamely. Keith always made him nervous, but he was playing it cool tonight. Clearly he was trying to impress his date.

"Hi, sweetie," I said, leaning in for a cheek kiss and half hug. "You look even more handsome than you did this afternoon. And, Bryce, can I say, you look quite dashing as well."

"Thanks, Mallory. I didn't even know you knew my name."

"Don't be silly, Bryce."

"I just meant we never really got to know each other here at school. And now that you're never here . . . Well, anyhow, I'm just babbling, aren't I?"

They were a cute couple, and it made me a little sad that Bryce was so nervous around me.

"Don't worry about it," I said. "Have you had a chance to dance yet?"

"Scooter doesn't dance."

"Well, we'll see what we can do about *that*."

My comment made Scooter blush fiercely. But I could tell that dancing was an inevitable part of his near future.

Keith then tugged at my arm. "My mom wants pictures. We should probably get in line."

I nodded and turned back to Scooter and Bryce. "You boys behave," I told them.

Scooter blushed even more.

The line for pictures took about half an hour. Keith and I amused ourselves by rating everyone's fashion choices. It got pretty wicked at times.

"Ooh, Patti Bishop, wearing an orange number ripe for Thanksgiving. It's like a kumquat on stilts."

I giggled. "And here comes Winnie Malcolm. A vision in copper and citrus. How long 'til she turns green with envy or rot?"

"Ah," Keith picked up, "and the loveliest gown of the evening is surely Kathy Klaustermeyer's. If only she didn't have to return it to the pound at the end of the night."

Keith and I burst out laughing. But then I realized maybe we'd been a bit too loud.

"You guys think you're so funny."

It was Amelia, clucking like an unamused chicken, dressed, appropriately enough, in a white, feathery number that made her look like the harlot of the henhouse.

"We're just entertaining ourselves while we wait in this endless photo line. I wish they had a fast pass like Disneyland," Keith said.

"You guys could be a little less rude about your fellow students. Honestly . . ."

I knew running into Amelia would be likely, but I had expected her to just shoot daggers at me with her eyes. I had not planned on an actual confrontation.

"Where's your hot date?" I asked.

"Right here, babe," said Jake as he emerged behind her.

Amelia tried to hide her embarrassment, but I could see right through her snide veneer.

"Brewster was injured at last night's match. Dislocated shoulder or something."

Before I could say I was sorry to hear about Brewster's injury, I was interrupted by Jake whooping like a maniac. It seemed his friends had just arrived, all in drag, and were making quite a scene. He ran over to them hollering, leaving his date/sister twisting in the wind. She seemed so pathetic in her molting gown.

"You two act like God's gift to *Seventeen* magazine readers. You're not any better than anyone else here."

And suddenly I realized: I was done being apologetic. I had tried, and I'd gotten a grape soda shower in response. It was time for us to both grow up.

"I didn't say that we were God's gift to anything. We were just commenting on clothes. You and I used to do it all the time."

"I don't think you're in any position to judge, Mallory. You're the one wearing hand-me-downs. I've seen your *mother* wear that dress."

"So what if she has?" I said. "I don't care. I'll bet Keith doesn't care."

Keith looked amused. "I truly, unabashedly, completely don't care."

"So it looks like you're the only one who cares, Amelia."

"Well, in a way it's appropriate," Amelia said. "You *should* be wearing your mother's clothes. After all, you're becoming *just like her.* Except she at least was decent enough to actually be famous before she turned into a total bitch."

This is how friends officially become enemies: when they take the thing they know will hurt you the most and use it against you.

"Shows how much you know!" I spat out. "She was *always* a bitch!"

I knew that wasn't the point. I wanted to slap her. In my mind, I was watching my hand fly through the air with Amelia's rouged cheek as its final destination. It made its connection with surprising force, and gave off the satisfying crackle of a good smack.

But I didn't do it. Because I didn't want to prove her point. I didn't want to be my mother.

There were other ways to hit her back.

"Amelia," I said calmly, "when the people at the network saw your audition tape, they actually laughed. When I told them I wanted to cast you, they said you would *sink the show*. You were that bad. And you can take it out on me all you want, but that doesn't mean you aren't a failed teen actress who couldn't even manage to get a part on the show her ex–best friend was writing. You may think I'm like my mother, but I'd rather be her than a retroactive has-been like you."

Amelia was stunned. So was Keith. Frankly, so was I. In this moment I had become just as nasty as my mother on her worst day. We all stood there in silence, trying to wrap our heads around what just happened. It was probably only a second or two, but it felt like eons.

"Let's go. We'll just wait for prom to take photos," Keith said decisively as he started to pull me away.

But before we could get out of the photo line (of fire), Amelia was suddenly airborne, flying at me in a hysterical rage, red-painted claws at the ready.

I tried to duck, but it was too late. Amelia pushed me hard, and I pushed back. She teetered on her heels, and we both went tumbling into the table and chairs behind us. The pink carnation centerpiece went clattering to the floor.

"Don't you *dare* insult me, you overrated TV princess!" Amelia screamed as she pulled at my hair, feathers flying everywhere from her dress. Fortunately my short new 'do made it hard for her to get a hold.

I stuck my hands in her face and tried to shove her off me, but she was strong. I didn't remember that about her.

"You can't blame me for blowing your audition!" I shouted.

"You promised me that role!" she screamed back. "You said it was mine!"

"Get some talent and we'll talk!"

By now a crowd had gathered around us. The loud music blared as we continued to roll around on the floor like something out of an Animal Planet wildlife special.

Finally Keith pulled her off me. But just as I was getting up, Amelia kicked out and connected her cheap pump with my right eye. I stumbled backward and fell to the floor again while Keith body-blocked Amelia.

I rubbed my eye while I slowly got to my feet. The last thing I had needed was a Nine West facial from Amelia. No teachers had noticed the skirmish. Or if they did, they didn't care. Keith was holding on to Amelia, keeping her away from me while I got my bearings.

"Let go of me, Keith."

"Calm down, Amelia," he said. "It's over."

"Oh, it sure is," she said. "But don't come crying to me when she finally dumps you for Dallas."

"What?" I said, turning red with fury again. How dare she?

"It's true, Keith. You're just a glorified seat filler on Emmy night. Mallory's had the hots for Dallas from the very first day she met him—as if that's not the most pathetic thing of all time. If he ever even *looks* in her direction, it'll be adios for you."

"Don't make me slap you," I warned. "I learned from the best."

"Just try it!" Amelia said through clenched teeth.

I almost did, but again thought better of it. If I've learned anything from soaps, it's to always leave them wanting more.

Finally Jake returned to the scene, and Amelia, suddenly self-conscious, fluffed her feathers and returned to the dance.

Keith and I headed to the nearest exit. I suppose we'd had enough fun for one evening. I kept apologizing, and Keith kept saying it wasn't my fault, although I sensed that he felt it was at least a quarter mine. We stopped at Scoops in Koreatown for some gourmet vegan ice cream, but there was no cherry on top of our conversation. I remembered those times my mother and one of my stepfathers would come home from a party or a premiere, and they wouldn't say a word to each other. He would take out his cuff links. She would kick off her shoes and make a drink. It was like they weren't in the same place anymore. The same room, yes, but in different dimensions.

This had been our one best chance at a great night, and I'd ruined it.

The ride to LAX was quiet. Keith didn't replay or comment on the event; in fact, he barely said anything except to ask which airline I was flying.

"Alaskan," I said softly. I pressed the ice-soaked napkin I was holding to my face, praying that I didn't have a black eye from my encounter with Amelia's foot.

Finally, just as Keith was approaching the airport, I decided to break the silence with another apology.

"I'm sorry for ruining the dance, Keith. I don't know what came over me." I put my hand on his leg and squeezed. "It's just, she knows what buttons to push, you know? Saying I'm just like my mother? She knew I'd react to that. She was looking for a fight."

"I don't doubt that," Keith said.

I didn't exactly think that my boyfriend would be *thrilled* with the fact that I'd gotten into a catfight (and not even over him!), but I didn't think he would be this quietly upset. It had to be the Dallas part.

"Don't believe anything Amelia said."

"Like what?"

"Like that thing about Dallas. You know we're just friends. Heck, we're barely even friends. We're co-workers on a good day. That's it."

"I saw the way you looked at him at dinner. You were worried that he was so down."

"Of course I was!" I exclaimed. "Because if he quits the show, we have no show!"

"The show, the show, the SHOW!!! I can't deal with hearing about it anymore. It's all you ever talk about!"

I sighed. "I'm sorry."

"We used to talk about so many other things. Like life. We used to talk about *life,* Mallory. Not opening credits or network vice presidents or what Alexis's lighting looked like on Thursday afternoon. I don't mind talking about those things, Mallory. Really, I don't. But they can't be *all* we talk about. The thing that just happened back there? You'd been holding that in for a long, long time. And I wish maybe you'd have shared a little of it with me. Because right now, I feel like I can't help—partly because I'm totally over my head, and partly because *you won't let me.*"

Just then we pulled up to the curb. I wanted to stay. I wanted to show Keith that Amelia was wrong—I loved him, not Dallas. I wanted to tell him that I was as sick of the show as he was, and that if I'd known what I was getting myself into, I never would have signed on. I wanted to tell him that

I wanted to run away together—maybe to Mexico. But I couldn't. I had a flight to catch. I had a job to do. I had a show to save.

"Can we talk about this tomorrow?" I asked.

"No. I need some time to think," he said. "We can talk on Monday."

My eyes started to mist again. I was not going to cry.

I took my suitcase out of the backseat. Then leaned back in.

"I do love you," I said, and kissed him on the cheek.

"I love you, too," he said. But there wasn't any happiness in it.

He pulled away from the curb, leaving me standing in my ruined hairstyle and ripped dress. As I waved goodbye, the Tiffany bracelet slid down my wrist, the heart a little smaller than it had seemed before.

He gave me a little hug, because he must
have known how much I needed it.
And he was right. I really needed it.

e i g h t e e n

It was a typically rainy night in the Northwest, which fit my mood perfectly. It wasn't pouring, but there was a relentless drizzle. I must have dozed off in the car that picked me up at the airport, because I was jolted awake by the squeal of brakes on wet asphalt when we arrived at the Deception Pass Lodge. A huge hulking mass of timber, this was where the cast and crew were staying. It was just after two in the morning when I got there, and the silence when I stepped out of the car was astounding. *Toto,* I wanted to say, *I don't think we're in Los Angeles anymore.*

There was one lone person in the lobby when I walked in: Greg, sitting and reading in an armchair that looked like it had been made from a buffalo. When I walked in, he looked up and gave me a big, sleepy smile.

"Greetings, traveler," he said. And I realized: He'd waited up for me. Just so I wouldn't be all alone this late at night in a strange place.

I suddenly understood the phrase *a sight for sore eyes.*

His expression turned to one of concern when he saw the torn dress I was wearing.

"Bad night?" he asked, standing up.

"You could say that," I replied.

"Must have been some dance."

"It was one for the record books. How are things up here?"

"Everyone arrived okay, and I think we're ready to go for tomorrow. There's something you should know, though—I'm not the only person Trip sent."

"Frieda Weiner?" I guessed.

Greg nodded. "She gave a little impromptu speech after dinner, 'on behalf of the network.' Basically, she told the cast to bring sexy back. And she looked at Dallas the whole time she said it."

"He must've been thrilled."

"Yeah, I think Francesca took his knife away so he wouldn't throw it or use it on himself."

Good girl, I thought.

"Richard was on the phone with your mom a lot; from his side of the conversation, it sounded like she was worried about not being in the opening credits reshoot. He kept telling her that her part was already set, and that it was only the 'amateurs' who needed reshoots. I think she liked that."

"She would."

Greg took a key from his pocket and handed it over to me.

"May I escort you to your room?" he asked.

"I'd be honored," I replied.

We caught up a little more as we walked through the lodge, but mostly we kept quiet so as not to wake our cast and crew.

"You know," he said as I opened my door, "it's really important whenever you go on a trip like this to have an escape spot. I already scouted one out—if you head out the exit by the dining room and follow the left path for about seven minutes, there's an outlook over the river. It's completely remote."

Perhaps this was what true friendship was: scouting out an escape spot and being willing to share it.

"Thank you," I said to Greg, unable to tell him how much I needed his easy kindness right now.

"My pleasure," he said. "Now get some sleep—it's going to be a crazy day tomorrow."

He gave me a little hug, because he must have known how much I needed it.

And he was right. I really needed it.

I thought about texting Keith, or even calling him in the morning to tell him I'd made it okay. But then I realized: a break was a break. If he wasn't going to call, I wasn't going to intrude.

I was still crying when I fell asleep.

Richard woke me up a few hours later to tell me that I needed to get myself down to the shooting location as soon as I could, so the two of us could plan out the shots. I was a little disgusted to see I'd fallen asleep in my dress, and was very happy to change out of it. When I opened my door, there was a breakfast tray waiting for me, with a good luck note from Greg. I drank my coffee like I was a car being pumped with gas, then demolished a few pastries on my way to the lobby. The first person I passed was Alexis, who had her usual smile plastered on her face. I used to think it was friendly, but now it seemed fake. I mumbled something to her with my croissant-filled mouth, then rushed forward so it wouldn't turn into a conversation.

Most of the cast was in the dining room. I peeked in and saw Francesca finishing the last bit of her egg whites and gulping orange juice. She was reading the *Seattle Post-Intelligencer* and looked annoyed. Across the room, under an assortment of taxidermy, was Dallas, picking at the buffet. He was wearing his sunglasses indoors. Never a good sign.

I ducked out before he could see me. Also not a good sign.

Richard and the crew were down at the black-sand beach beneath the Deception Pass bridge. There was a van waiting to shuttle me down there. It felt silly, and fitting, to be riding in the van alone.

"Have you seen our cast?" I asked Richard when I found him sitting on a rock near where the crew was setting up. "They look a little beaten down."

"That's what makeup is for. They'll look fine once they get bronzed," he said dismissively.

"I hear Frieda Weiner, network consultant, gave them a little pep talk last night."

"I say this with all due respect," Richard said, "but if there'd been a trapdoor under that woman, I would have opened it. Without hesitation."

That made me feel better. In a twisted way, the one thing I could count on from Richard was the truth. I'd talked to my agent, Donald, about this, and he'd said, "When it comes to bull, trust your nose." He'd also said he'd talk to Trip if things got bad, but I wanted to go to the mat on my own for now.

"Can we keep her away from the shoot?" I asked.

Richard shook his head. "That's a negative. Trip gave her the search warrant, so we can't bar the door."

He handed me a few pieces of paper that laid out all the shots we were planning to get over the next two days. I scanned them and immediately started making them better.

"Why is Alexis in a bikini again? It's twenty degrees up here and the sun shines like four days out of the year. No one wears *bikinis* in Deception Pass."

"I think we might be able to fight off the bikinis, Mallory, but you'll probably have to show a little skin somewhere else."

"I'm not opposed to characters taking their clothes off *as long as it makes sense.*"

We figured out the rest of the changes by the time the van returned . . . this time carrying the cast, and Frieda Weiner.

"That was a lovely party yesterday," Richard said, out of the blue. "Your mother really knows how to get what she wants."

Yeah, I thought. *Even if it means conspiring against her own daughter.*

But I didn't say anything . . . because even though I knew he was telling me the truth about the network, I still wasn't sure which side he was on when it came to Alexis and my mother.

To my surprise, the day's shoot started off pretty well. We spent the waking hours going from setup to setup on and around the bridge. We shot Javier's beauty shots first. Then Alexis did an admirable job of projecting innocent, doe-eyed expressions that also projected a sultry inner life. From the way she tilted her jaw to the camera and looked up under her eyebrows, I knew my mother had been giving her pointers.

That left us with Dallas. When he arrived on set, everything seemed fine. He was in a wet suit and looking, I might add, *damn fine*. His attitude left something to be desired, though it seemed to warm when he learned I was in charge. We got off the first few shots of Dallas walking down the beach, framed gorgeously by the rising peaks of the surrounding mountains. The sun was just behind him, giving his hair that ethereal glow one associates with the angel Gabriel.

"That sound you hear is the sound of a million teenage girls falling in love," one of the camera operators joked.

For me, it didn't feel like a joke.

Even Richard seemed pleased.

"I think you've captured it," he said. And I was a little relieved that I wasn't the only one who was seeing it.

The only person who didn't seem to get it was Frieda Weiner.

"That's nice," she said, "but I think we should try it shirtless, too."

"I don't think that's necessary," I said, remembering what had happened at the photo shoot.

"Oh, but I do," Frieda Weiner said with the falsest smile she could muster. "We don't have to use it, but I want to try it."

"Sounds fair to me," Richard chimed in.

But Dallas doesn't want to take his shirt off, I wanted to say. And then I realized: That was a pretty lame reason not to try the shot. I couldn't spend my whole time on the show defending

Dallas, especially when I knew what the audience wanted: sexy boys wearing next to nothing. Alexis in a bikini made no sense, storywise. But Dallas with his shirt off kind of did. We had to see why Sarah and Jacqueline were so attracted to Ryan—and this would be a way to do it in the opening credits.

Everyone was looking at me now. Richard. Frieda. Francesca. Alexis. Javier. The crew. And Dallas. I tried to read the expression on his face, but it was a closed book.

"Fine," I said. "But just because we tape it doesn't mean we'll use it."

I could tell from the look on Francesca's face that I'd made the wrong choice. But Dallas—well, suddenly Dallas looked happy. Or, at the very least, mischievous. Coyly, he reached for the zipper of his wet suit.

"You sure?" he asked.

I nodded.

Dallas unzipped the wet suit, and at first there was just the barest line of skin exposed. The zipper went all the way down, and I realized I had no idea what he was wearing underneath. If anything.

I couldn't help but think of what Javier had said before.

Oh, honey, I've already seen it in wardrobe a hundred times. And let me tell you, he has hair in all *the right places.*

There it was, that glimpse of chest hair. Then Dallas was unzipped, and he started to pull the wet suit off his shoulders.

I forgot to breathe.

There they were—his shoulders, his chest, just the right amount of hair, and . . . writing.

Yes, writing.

Black marker writing. All across his torso. Scrawled.

THIS BODY WASN'T MEANT TO SELL
TV SHOWS.

I'M NOT YOUR OBJECT.

IF YOU'RE READING THIS, I SHOULD
BE HOME BY NOW.

Some of the crew laughed. Alexis giggled nervously. Francesca shook her head. Frieda's lips pursed into a straight line that was tighter than her last face-lift. Javier stared and fumbled for his camera phone.

Dallas had stopped unzipping at his waist.

"Do you want me to continue?" he asked, looking straight at Frieda Weiner.

"No," she said. "I think that's more than enough."

I was relieved that he'd asked her the question, not me. But after he zipped the wet suit back on, he shot me a look that was pure disappointment. I'd given in again, and had sold him out. The rejection might have been for Frieda Weiner, but the writing—well, the writing had been for me.

And now Richard was looking at me. And his meaning was clear: *You wanted to be in charge, so now you are in charge, and the next move is yours. How are you going to handle this?*

"What the hell are you doing?" I bellowed at the top of my lungs. I didn't need the megaphone to be heard.

Dallas looked surprised, then shrugged. "Sorry, I got a little upset last night. I wasn't thinking."

I shook my head in despair. I thought about my options. I could get Javier back in for a chest shot. I was sure he'd jump at the chance to display his wares, but it all seemed pointless now.

"Dallas, why are you working so hard to sabotage this show?"

I asked this calmly, not at all hysterical. Dallas started to respond, as if to explain himself, but then he clammed up. Instead, he said coldly, "Are we going to do this or not?"

"We're not going to do this," I said. "Any of it." I turned around to face the crew. "We're moving on, folks. Let's set up Francesca now."

When I turned back to face Dallas to try and figure out what on earth was going through his head, I found that he had already started back to the van. Alexis ran after him, which only pissed off Francesca more.

"Thanks, Dallas!" I shouted out.

He stopped in his tracks and looked back. He looked really sad and defeated. He looked a lot like I felt.

But I had more shots to get in the can and we were losing the light. No time for mourning now.

n i n e t e e n

The rest of the shooting went as well as it could. For whatever reason, Frieda Weiner wasn't as adamant on sexing Francesca up, so she stopped interfering. Richard and I even had time to scout out some scenes for future exterior shots, in case the network would let us go back on location.

I was exhausted when we were through. Dinner was being served in the dining room, but I ordered room service instead. I didn't want to see Dallas, and the thought of a conversation with the cloying Alexis made me nauseous. In the few moments when I stopped thinking about the show, I thought instead about how Keith was probably going to break up with me when I got home. My whole life was going down the drain and I hadn't even taken the SATs yet.

I was about to fall asleep while watching PBS when my room phone rang. It was Javier.

"Hey, girl, whatcha doing?"

"Writing a suicide note," I replied dryly.

"Is it good?"

"Getting there."

"You've been holed up in your room all night. Why don't you come to my room? We can watch *Saturday Night Live* together."

"I don't know, Javier. I'm zonked," I said, rubbing my eyes.

"Come on. Let's have some girl talk."

I guess it wasn't doing me any good to sit alone in my room sulking and feeling sorry for myself. So I agreed.

A few minutes later I found myself knocking on Javier's door. He opened the door with a goofy grin.

"Hey-y-y," he said. "Come on in."

Somehow, Javier had managed to make his lodge room look like he'd lived in it for months . . . and hadn't cleaned once. It also had the herbal scent of my second stepfather's "meditation room." He gestured for me to have a seat on the bed, then cleared off his American Apparel briefs so I would feel at home.

"Long day, huh?" he asked as he flopped on the bed beside me. "Dallas is quite the downer. Although now it seems like he's got company."

"Company?" I asked.

"Yeah. He's next door. And it sounds like there's a love scene going on."

He grabbed a water glass from his nightstand and handed me one from the bathroom sink. He put his up to the wall and started listening more closely, but I refrained.

"I think they're talking dirty to each other."

"Who?"

"I guess Dallas and Francesca are back together."

"They are!?" I exclaimed. I put my glass to the wall, but all I could hear were murmurs. A boy murmur and a girl murmur.

"I guess she's not mad anymore," I said.

"Who could stay mad at a hunk like that?" Javier asked rhetorically.

There was a knock at the door.

Javier went to open it. Greg was standing there, looking like he'd just spent some quality time fixing himself up.

"Hey!" he said to Javier. Then he saw me in the room and looked confused.

"Mallory!" he covered quickly. "I didn't know you were here!"

He walked in and hovered awkwardly. I noticed that Javier didn't gesture for him to sit down the way he had with me.

"What're you doing?" Greg asked.

"Spying on Dallas and Francesca," Javier answered.

The phone rang. Javier looked surprised when he heard the voice on the other end, then said to come on over.

"Who was that?" I asked.

"You'll see," he teased.

A minute later, there was another knock.

"Well, well, well," Javier said as he answered it. "If it isn't our raven-haired beauty."

In pranced Francesca, looking fresh and friendly. "What's going on, guys?"

"Wait a minute," I said, pressing my ear again to the wall of Dallas's suite. "If you're here, who's in there?"

For some reason neither Francesca, Greg, Javier, nor I was able to wrap our heads around the obvious.

"We've got to find out!" Javier said. And that's how Greg and I each came to be holding on to one of Javier's legs while he dangled over his balcony to see inside Dallas's window.

"If you told me yesterday I'd be re-enacting some Three Stooges maneuver in order to spy on Dallas, I wouldn't have believed you," I said to Greg as we strained to keep Javier from falling two stories into the bushes.

"Beats watching J.Lo in *Maid in Manhattan,* which is what I was doing before this," Francesca said with a wee bit of ice in her voice.

"I think syphilis beats that movie," Greg huffed.

We returned our full attention to Javier as he tried to perform his Mission: Impossible.

"Can you see anything?" I whispered.

"Almost," he said as he inched himself farther over the railing. "This is a hell of an abs workout." Then he gasped. "Pull me back, pull me back!"

Greg and I tumbled backward, pulling Javier with us. We all ended up in a heap at Francesca's feet.

"So? What did you see?" she asked, with the kind of chill that turns waterfalls into icicles and men into castrati.

Javier took a deep breath. "Dallas is in there, all right. And he's not alone."

"Who's with him?" I asked.

"Alexis," said Francesca. "It's Alexis, isn't it?"

Javier nodded. "And Bingo was his name-oh."

"They could be rehearsing," I said. "You know, a love scene. If only we could hear what they're saying . . ."

"Well, it had moved a little beyond talking, if you know what I mean," Javier said, enjoying himself thoroughly.

I wasn't at all prepared for this.

"I guess he's finally made new friends," I said to Francesca. She shook her head. "Not the ones I wanted."

I touched her arm in a vague sign of female solidarity.

Suddenly, we heard the door to his room open—then close.

"Was that a slam?" Javier asked.

"No," Francesca said. "That was just a goodbye."

"Drama!" Javier proclaimed. But he seemed to be the only one in the mood for it. Sensing this, he said, "I'm thinking the party's over?"

"Did it ever really start?" Greg asked. Something was clearly bothering him.

"Are you going to talk to Dallas?" I asked Francesca.

"No," she said. "Why would I? He can make his own mistakes."

Before I could ask if she was okay, she was making excuses and leaving.

Javier yawned.

"We get the hint," Greg said.

"Thanks for a great time," I added. "And the use of your glasses."

"Hey! It's not my fault Romeo over there decided to show Juliet the writing on his bod."

Just the mention of Romeo made my heart break a little wider, and I found myself falling into the gap that the break had caused.

"Escape spot?" I asked Greg as we left Javier's room.

"Escape spot," he replied.

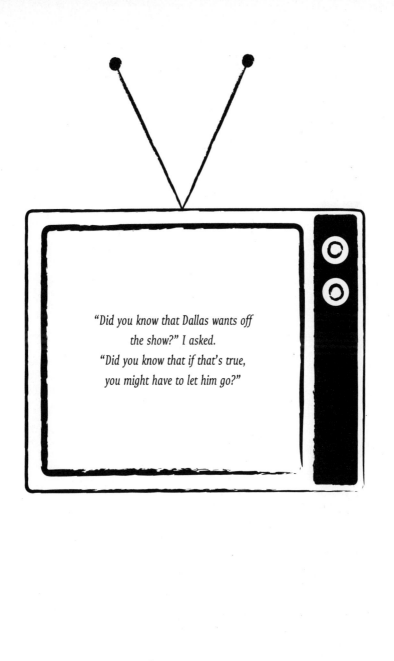

"Did you know that Dallas wants off
the show?" I asked.
"Did you know that if that's true,
you might have to let him go?"

t w e n t y

The escape spot was exactly what the name promised: a deep pause in the world, away from lights and voices. We walked there in silence, and at first we stayed there in silence, guarded by the trees and the unseen river that ran beneath the overlook. There was a wooden railing meant to keep us from falling, but it seemed beside the point. Anyone who wanted to jump could still jump. And anyone who wanted to stay could still stay.

"Did you know that I haven't even graduated college?" Greg asked, looking out into the darkness. "I started interning at the network when I was a sophomore, and they convinced me to stay. I take night classes so I can eventually get my diploma."

"Did you know that I've lost pretty much all of my high school friends?" I asked him back. "Not just Amelia. All the other girls who came with the territory, who I thought were friends. When the territory changed, they went with it."

"Did you know that I still live at home?" Greg said, still staring out into the unknown. "Did you know that I have to leave my house at five in the morning every day and that I usually come home at midnight?"

"Did you know that my middle name is Sarah?"

"Did you know that my middle name is Percy?"

I laughed. "Percy?"

He looked at me. "Don't ask."

"Did you know that my boyfriend is about to break up with me over this show?"

"Did you know that I like both girls and boys?"

This one seemed to require an answer. "I didn't know that," I said. "But that's cool."

"Did you know that I kissed Javier last night, and that he then told me it was probably a mistake?"

Now I understood what had just happened. Greg had thought he was getting a second chance, but he wasn't.

"Did you know that you deserve much, much more than a guy like Javier?" I asked.

"Did you know that even if I did know I deserve more than that, it still haunts me that I can't at least have it?"

I stepped closer to him and leaned on his shoulder. I could hear the river now.

"Did you know that I'm a total mess?" I asked.

"Did you know you're not alone?"

"Did you know I'm probably in love with two guys at the same time? I mean, I know that's not allowed. But it's how I feel. I honestly don't know what to do. I love Keith. But just now, when Dallas was with Alexis—it wouldn't have hurt me so much if I wasn't feeling something for him. None of it would hurt so much."

He leaned his head on top of mine.

"Did you know it's not completely crazy for you to be in love with two guys at the same time?"

"But I have to choose, right?"

I felt him nod. "Yes, you'll have to choose. Or the choice will be made for you. And by that point the choice is usually neither."

Was that what Keith was doing—making the choice for me? Was that what I wanted?

"Did you know that Dallas wants off the show?" I asked.

"Did you know that if that's true, you might have to let him go?"

"Did you know that I'm not ready to face that?"

"Did you know you might not have any alternative?"

"Did you know you smell nice?"

"Did you know that's just deodorant?"

"Did you know I don't care?"

"Did you know how glad I am you don't care?"

I reached my arm around him.

"Did you know how glad I am that you're here?" I asked.

He moved his arm around me. "Did you know how glad I am that *you're* here?"

This is, I suppose, another thing about escape spots: They give you a clearing so you can say to yourself, *Okay, I can do this.*

If I didn't know that before, I did now.

I didn't ask Francesca.
This was one decision I was going to
have to make on my own.

twenty-one

Except for a reassuring warmth between me and Greg, on-set relations went arctic the next day. No one spoke much. Dallas was withdrawn. Francesca was a paler version of herself, as if all the caring had been drained right out. On top of that, she barely ever came within fifty yards of Dallas. Trying to wrangle her into a group shot was like chasing a lizard blindfolded.

Alexis, on the other hand, was *always* looking at Dallas. He didn't seem to notice. Typical guy. Javier was the only one in a mildly cheery mood, and I'm pretty sure that's just because he loved the drama of it all. And he was only too happy to take his shirt off. "This one's for you, Greg," he joked at one point. Greg seemed mortified, and as punishment I made Javier shoot his next few shirtless shots in the freezing water underneath the bridge.

We managed to get most of the shots I wanted, which is a rarity on any set, let alone one as chronically dysfunctional as ours. Bizarrely, Dallas's broodiness worked in the group shots, and the body tension between him, Francesca, and Alexis was palpable.

"I don't know what's going on," Richard said, "but it's working."

For a second, I wondered if he'd planned it all.

Frieda Weiner kept muttering about Dallas's attitude problem, and when she called Trip to check in, she made sure to tell him about that. (Since Greg had to put all the calls through, I had a direct line to their conversations.)

I avoided having any moments alone with Dallas, and he seemed to be avoiding having moments alone with me. I had no idea what he was thinking anymore, and I was torn between caring and feeling like I shouldn't care at all.

In other words: He was still having an effect on me. I just didn't know what it meant.

We made it to the airport in plenty of time for our flight back. When we landed at LAX, Francesca offered to take me home. I wasn't really in the mood to talk to anyone. We'd all been silent on the flight back, our noses buried in books or *Us Weekly*. But it sounded better than a cab. Keith was supposed to have picked me up, but he had texted on Sunday afternoon to say he couldn't make it—the one message I got from him the whole weekend. I didn't take that as a good sign.

Once Francesca and I found her Prius in short-term parking, we started the slow crawl through LA traffic. The drive was as depressing as the weekend.

I was staring out the window at the Hummers on Sepulveda when I finally turned to Francesca and said, "Dallas is trying to get fired, isn't he?"

"It would seem so."

"What are we going to do about it?"

"Fire him."

"What? Are you serious? We can't fire Dallas. You yourself said he was our star. We can't let him go. We have too much invested," I argued.

"Mal, he's been acting like a spoiled brat for the past week and it's getting worse. I have no idea whether his hotel-room antics with Alexis were part of that or whether he genuinely wanted to make out with her. But that's almost beside the point. He's actively sabotaging the show now, not just his own career. I won't go down for that self-obsessed artiste, no matter how talented he is. Neither should you. It's definitely not your fault that he signed his next few **years** away before Shakespeare came calling. I thought Dallas could work through it, but clearly he can't."

I was shocked to hear Francesca talk this way about Dallas. I had expected her to suggest mediation, not a full-blown attack. Was it her jealousy of Alexis talking, or did she really mean it?

I thought back to that magical day at the Getty when we first met. It had seemed like a match made in heaven. Could things have really soured so fast?

Or did he want me to put up a fight to keep him? Wouldn't that show him that he really mattered?

I didn't ask Francesca.

This was one decision I was going to have to make on my own.

Francesca dropped me off at home. My mother was out. I was relieved. That way I didn't have to explain the ruined dress right off the bat.

I climbed into my bed and clicked on E! Just as I was dozing off, about to dream of a world without decisions, the doorbell rang. I went to the intercom and pressed speak.

"Hello?"

"Mallory? It's Keith," said the voice.

Keith? What was he doing here? I wasn't ready to deal with him yet. But I guess when there's an avalanche, you can't be surprised that the rocks keep falling.

He was already on the porch when I opened the door.

"Hi," I said. "This is unexpected. I figured you didn't want to see me when you said you couldn't pick me up from the airport."

"Sorry if driving in circles around LAX waiting for you to land didn't fit into my work schedule," Keith said bleakly. As usual, he looked spectacular. A rare February heat wave had hit the Southland and the temperature, even at this late hour, was hovering somewhere around eighty degrees. Keith was dressed in his black zippered bondage shorts that hung below the knee with various straps hooking every which way. He wore a Cheap Trick shirt that was ripped ever so elegantly just above his left shoulder, revealing the subtle contours of his collarbone. His mussed hair fell over his eyes, which were looking at his sandals. He flexed his toes.

"Come in," I said. "My mom's not home."

"No?" Keith said, perking up. "Where is she?"

"Who knows? I got back and she wasn't here."

He followed me into the living room and I tried for small talk, asking how his weekend was. He was not terribly responsive. I didn't know what to do.

"Want to take a dip in the Jacuzzi?" I asked.

He shook his head. "I don't think this is a Jacuzzi moment."

Instead we headed over to the couch in the living room. He sat next to me, but not too close.

"I've been thinking . . . ," he said slowly.

"About?"

"About us."

"Are you here to break up with me?" I said evenly.

Keith sighed. "I don't want to. But I'm thinking that I can't see a solution for us. I'm not sure if I'm ready to become a stay-at-home boyfriend who just waits for you to tell me how your day was."

He was right. I couldn't deny that. But I wasn't about to give up this easily. Keith was the one thing I wanted before any of this *Likely Story* stuff started happening.

"Does this have anything to do with the lies Amelia was spinning about Dallas?" I had to ask.

"I do believe you, Mallory. I really do. But . . ."

"But what? You either believe me or you don't."

"It isn't that easy. Dallas represents, rightly or wrongly, all the problems with our relationship. Even if you don't like him, it's going to kill me to think about the two of you spending every day together when I'm lucky to get half an hour with you at eleven o'clock at night."

I moved toward him and stroked his face. "What can I do to fix this?"

"I don't think there is anything. I hate to say this, Mallory, but I think this is over. We tried. You can't say we didn't. . . ."

He took my hand and kissed it. It felt like the promise of a life not lived.

Keith lifted himself from the couch. He just stood there looking at me.

"Goodbye, Mallory," he said with a gulp. "I'll see you around."

He started to walk away.

"Wait!"

He turned around and faced me as I chased after him.

"I'll fire Dallas!" I found myself saying.

"What?" he said, confused.

"You heard me. I'll fire Dallas. Will that prove how much I value this—how much I value *us*? I'm not going to stand here and promise to be better or promise to change. I've already done that and it's still led us here. I'll fire Dallas tomorrow to prove to you how much you mean to me. He's gone. Do you hear me? He's gone."

A pause extended for what felt like two minutes. Finally, Keith said quietly, "Can you do that?"

I smiled and embraced him. "For you, anything."

And then we kissed, and kissed, and kissed until my mother came home.

I could keep what I wanted, and give Dallas what he wanted, too.

twenty-two

Keith left shortly after my mother returned. She halfheartedly asked me how the shoot went, and I told her it was fine. I didn't bother to ask where she'd been.

I spent the rest of the night writing the death of Dallas's character. I took the easy way out and killed him with a knife to the back. It was a pretty standard-issue soap death. (You didn't want to go decapitating or burning them because you never knew when they'd get written back in.)

In the wee small hours of the morning I managed to draft a pretty respectable sequence. Sarah and Ryan would have a horrendous fight. Then Ryan would storm out into the cold, dark night. The wind blows and the rain patters the fern groves. Ryan hears a sound. Is he being watched? Back in the house, Sarah realizes she was too hasty and decides to go after him. But it's dark—where did he go?

It's then that she sees something. Or someone? It's hard to tell, but her gut tells her something's wrong. She calls out for Ryan. He calls back just as lightning illuminates the scene and we see a hooded figure about to put a knife into Ryan's back. *"Look out!"* she screams . . . but it's too late. Ryan starts to walk back to his beloved Sarah, but a dagger plunges into his perfectly chiseled frame and he gurgles blood as thunderclaps resound in the night.

Terrified, Sarah runs to him. The killer is gone. But Ryan lies bleeding. It is there, in Sarah's arms, that the ravaged and rain-drenched Ryan breathes his last breath. It's tragic. It's heart-wrenching. It's character-defining. (Well, for Sarah, at least. For Ryan, it's character-ending.)

It wasn't hard to figure out who was doing the knife-plunging. Since we had an anonymous murderer residing in Deception Pass, it seemed like I might as well put him to work. Before, he'd just killed a character that didn't even exist. If a major character was killed, it would mean something. Nobody would be expecting it. The press coverage would be amazing. Killing off the lead in the first month! The audience would *care.*

Or so I told myself.

Unsurprisingly, I was dreading my arrival at the studio the next morning. For once, though, it wasn't Richard I was hoping to avoid. I knew he'd be pissy about axing Dallas, pretending it was a huge inconvenience, but I hoped that secretly he'd be thrilled. He'd think it would be easy to replace him—just call central casting and get the latest hunk of the month. I doubted we'd ever strike black gold again like we did with Dallas . . . but it was a risk I had to take.

The person I really didn't want to confront was Dallas. It wasn't that I thought he'd be upset. I just wished I could have seen this coming. I might have been able to do something more than pull the plug. We were supposed to have taken the world by storm together. We were supposed to have been friends. But everything had gone wrong.

I found him in his dressing room. The door was open, and I looked for a moment at the posters of the Juilliard shows he'd starred in—*Godspell*, *The Dark at the Top of the Stairs*, *Steel Magnolias*. Books and scripts were piled up in the corners, and I wondered if any of them were *Romeo and Juliet*.

I poked in my head and asked, "Can we talk for a second?"

"Sure," Dallas said, hopping up from his seat and clearing a place at the table. "I've been meaning to talk to you."

I sat down and presented a serious look while I folded my hands on his table much the way my mother acts "listening" when she's playing the guidance counselor.

"What do you want to talk about?" I asked.

"You first."

"Alrighty, me first. I don't think I have to be a genius to know that you're unhappy."

"You could say that," he said, blowing a lock of hair out of his face with a sharp burst of air.

"I'm sorry for that. I didn't expect it to turn out this way. The network promised me so much more power than I've ended up with. I'm fighting—you know that—but it's not easy and it's certainly not easy with my actors undermining me, too."

Dallas looked surprised. "I'm not undermining you," he said.

"What do you call that Magic Marker stunt?"

"Artistic expression?"

I shook my head. "Look, I get it. You don't like what we're doing, so you're hoping to get fired. Well, congratulations. You're dead."

I tossed the script onto the table between us.

"What's this?" Dallas asked, not touching it.

"Your funeral. Ryan is going to get murdered by the Deception Pass Serial Killer. You'll only have one more week on the set, tops."

"Wow," he said weakly. Like me, once he got what he wanted, he seemed to wonder why he'd wanted it in the first place.

"So, that's my news. What did you want to talk about?"

Dallas picked up the script, but didn't open it. Then he looked up at the clock that ticked away incessantly in the background.

"I'm due on set," he finally said. "Can we talk later?"

"Sure. But I'm only here until lunch today 'cause I've scheduled school for the afternoon."

And with that, I left his dressing room. I wasn't happy, but I was relieved. The dirty deed was done, and he'd seemed to take it well. Had he put up a fight—had he told me he wanted to stay—I probably would have thrown the script in the garbage. But he hadn't put up a fight, and he hadn't told me he wanted to stay. So there was no going back.

"You're my goddess!" Richard said when I broke the news. "This calls for a celebration. I'm having a full-flavor Coca-Cola Classic—none of that diet NutraSweet swill today."

This was not the reaction I'd been expecting.

"You are really coming into your own, Mallory. Coke Classic?"

"Sure," I said. He cracked his soda open, then handed me one with a straw and lemon.

"I'm serious—this was a really great decision. We had to get rid of him. I just didn't think you had it in you to pull the lever on the guillotine."

"But what was all that stuff on the set about renewing his contract just to watch him lie in a coffin?" I asked. "I kind of thought you'd be furious."

Richard sighed a Mr. Miyagi sigh. It's like I was the fifth Karate Kid and while I'd learned one maneuver, I was still a long way off from that black belt and I'd probably never be Ralph Macchio.

"I said that to protect *you*, Mallory."

"You did?" I asked incredulously.

"I knew Dallas would be trouble the first time I saw his head shot. He's got the kind of ego that makes him think he has something to give back to the world through his acting. It's hard to defuse that."

"Then why did you let me hire him?" I interjected, sipping my Coke through the straw. The lemon really brought out the flavor. I'd have to remember that trick.

"Because you were infatuated and I was willing to take a chance. We all saw his X factor. Yet, unfortunately, he wasn't a team player. You saw the spark in Dallas and you knew to grab for it even if it might burn. Getting rid of him is even smarter, and killing him off is the most brilliant stroke of all. That will generate headlines, I guarantee you. You knew to cut him loose before he became an even bigger liability. If he'd broken out, it would have been impossible to fire him. By doing it now, we have shock *and* awe."

I certainly felt the shock.

This was really happening.

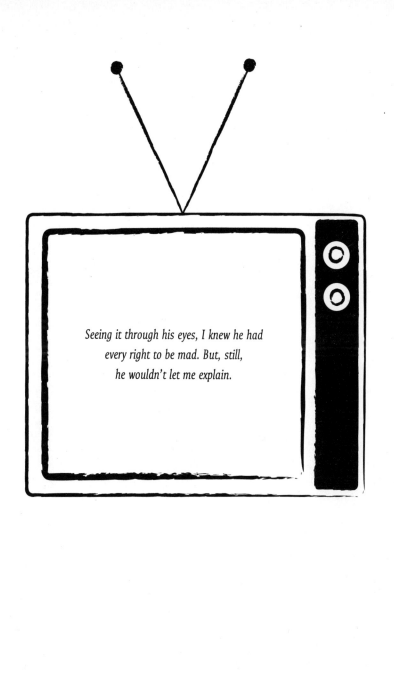

*Seeing it through his eyes, I knew he had
every right to be mad. But, still,
he wouldn't let me explain.*

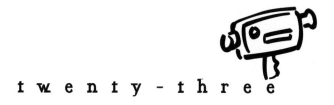

twenty-three

I spent the afternoon reading *Anna Karenina* for AP English. Miss Julie had a headache, so I was tackling Tolstoy in the comfort of my own home. Exasperated at the book's length and tiny print, I was just about ready to shove her onto the train tracks myself when my doorbell rang. My mother was still at the set. The video feed from the camera near the gate wasn't working for some reason, so I had to go downstairs and peer through the front window to see who had buzzed.

I couldn't quite make out who was standing there. Today had been sacked by a wet fog—especially up here in the hills over Hollywood. I grabbed a hoodie and scuttled down the drive.

I stopped in my tracks when I first saw Dallas's locks curling out from underneath his Dodgers cap. I continued on, reminding myself that Dallas was not Amelia, and the chances of me being pushed backward into a non-heated pool were therefore greatly reduced.

The evergreens surrounding our gate and driveway dripped with dew.

"Dallas?"

He looked up at me and adjusted his cap anxiously. "Hey, boss. I'm sorry to show up unannounced, but . . . well, I was hoping we could talk."

I nodded and opened the gate to let him in.

In the kitchen, I made some coffee with this new mocha mix my mother had been given in yet another gift basket. It was sort of like hot chocolate with an extra kick.

Dallas was sitting at the table, his skin glowing with the warm light reflecting off of the brass pots. I set the mug down in front of him and took a seat.

"So what's up?" I asked.

Dallas sighed. "I've been trying to figure out all day what it is I want to say to you."

"Any luck?"

He shook his head. "Not really. You know, when you do this much acting all the time, you get really used to delivering crisp little speeches. Things are so concise. But I'm having a hard time keeping track of all the different things I want to communicate."

"Join the club," I said, still a bit weary from *Anna K.*

"So let me start here. I'm super-sorry for my recent behavior. I don't know what got into me. I've never acted like that with anyone. Not even my parents. Well, maybe with my parents, but . . . my point is, I don't know what got into me. It's this show, Mallory. It's so much pressure. There's so much work and it never ends. There's always another scene, always another day. I'm not even twenty and I'm getting ulcers."

"You are?" I said, surprised.

"I don't know—it feels like it sometimes."

I knew that feeling. The feeling that my stomach was eating itself from the inside out. It wasn't hunger; instead, it burned like hot coals. I took Dallas's hand in a sign of solidarity and empathy.

"I get it," I told him quietly. "This show has changed everything for the worse. I have no time for friends, for fun. I don't even have time for schoolwork. No wonder people in this town are so stupid—they don't have time to learn anything. I can only imagine it's been worse for you, making the cross-continental move and ending up here with no time for yourself."

I was still holding his hand. And now he was holding my hand back.

Suddenly the thought of him and Alexis flashed through my head.

I let go of his hand.

"Is the script final?" he asked.

"More or less. Why? You don't like it? I thought a knife plunge was kind of sexy. It's very Now," I said, unsure of what he was asking.

"Stabbings are very Now?" he asked incredulously.

"Well," I stalled, suddenly realizing how dumb that sounded, "I guess we could say that knifings never go out of style on soap operas. It's like the little black dress of murders."

"I think there's been a misunderstanding. I never really wanted to quit," Dallas said.

"What?" I was floored. "You've been doing everything possible to get fired. Sabotaging shoots, fighting with the execs, sleeping with your castmates . . ."

"What?" Dallas said this time. He was white as a Miami hotel room. "What are you saying?"

That last comment had slipped out. I wanted to backtrack, but knew that I couldn't.

"We know, Dallas. Javier, Francesca, and I—we know about you and Alexis."

"How?" he asked, wanting answers.

I was not about to admit to our little covert operation, so I decided not to answer.

"We just know. That lodge wasn't as spacious as it seemed."

Dallas was over by the counter now, pacing back and forth. "I know that this doesn't really help matters, but I didn't sleep with her. I only kissed her that one time, and it was only because our characters were supposed to be in love, and I just wasn't feeling it when we were acting. I thought if maybe I felt something for Alexis, then Ryan would feel something for Sarah."

Dallas was right. That didn't help.

"This is all beside the point," I said dismissively, because if he went on about it more, it would only get worse. "What were you saying about the misunderstanding?"

Dallas put his hands on his forehead and ran them through his hair as he collected his thoughts.

"I was trying to be your Gandhi."

Actors. It's like they speak their own language. It sounds like English, but it doesn't make any sense.

Before I was forced to ask for a clarification as to how, exactly, Dallas was in any way like Gandhi, he continued. "I was trying that whole nonviolent protest thing. I figured if I threw my weight behind you, the network would have to return your creative control. But things kind of backfired and I guess I ended up messing you up more than Richard or Frieda Weiner or the network. I just wanted them to follow through on their promise to let you have your show. Otherwise, why are we doing this? We signed on to do something of our own, not a retread of every other show that's ever been on."

I didn't really know how to respond.

"So what are you saying, Dallas?" I asked.

He took a breath. "I like you, Mallory. I really, really like you. And I used to like this show. I'm sorry it all went down this way. It's not what I wanted. I wish we could start all over."

"Me too," I said to him, and then, more to myself, "Me too."

Dallas stepped closer to me, close enough for me to feel his hot breath on my neck. He was invading my personal space, but somehow I didn't mind, like he was D-Day and I was Normandy. *Storm me,* I thought. It sent a quick shiver down my spine. I had to tilt my head up to look at him.

Suddenly, he seemed to become aware of our unnatural proximity and he backed away. He nervously ran his hand through his hair again and said, "I've got to get going."

"Yeah, you probably should," I said, breaking the lingering trance. "I'll walk you out."

The afternoon had turned from damp to wet. I put the hood up on my sweatshirt as Dallas and I dashed down the driveway. The rain was cold and the wind had picked up. It blew the drops straight into our faces, but it felt good against my still-blushing cheeks.

I punched the code to open the gate. When his path was finally clear of wrought iron and steel, Dallas strode out of the gate and presumably out of my life forever. Sure, there would be a few days remaining on the set. But then he'd be off to New York, and I'd still be here. We'd never be together again.

I took a breath. *Get a hold of yourself, Mallory,* I thought. *You've got to stop letting yourself get all moon-eyed every time he comes within ten feet of you.*

He wants to leave.

Let him leave.

Dallas turned around to face me. He started walking back toward me.

"Can I have a hug?" he asked.

I nodded. And then I embraced him.

When his mouth made its way to my ear, he said something I wasn't expecting.

"Don't kill me, Mallory. Let's fix this show. We've been working against each other, but now we can work together. We can save both the show and our integrity."

"How?" I asked. "How do we get it back?"

"You're the boss. You tell me."

I was just about to tell him he was crazy, that we'd never get it back and that it wasn't worth trying. Integrity was for suckers in this town. I was just about to pull away from his embrace and walk back into the house to face Anna Karenina and her lousy lot. But before I could do any of those sensible things, the worst possible thing happened: I heard the familiar guitar chords of Tom Petty and I knew without having to look that Keith had just pulled up to discover me in the arms of another boy.

Needless to say, he wasn't pleased.

I looked him right in the eye and said, "I promise."
It felt wrong. But the alternative seemed more wrong.

twenty-four

"What the hell was *he* doing here, Mallory?"

Keith was fuming. And, seeing it through his eyes, I knew he had every right to be mad. But, still, he wouldn't let me explain.

"Calm down!" I yelled, slamming the front door behind me.

Dallas had made a quick exit after Keith arrived. He didn't leave me in the lurch—it was clear he would have stayed to fight it out with Keith if he'd had to—but that was the last thing I'd wanted. So I'd told him to go. And he'd gone, leaving me with Keith and his suspicions. Admirably, Keith had said little to nothing in front of Dallas. He was clearly saving it for me.

"Just last night you said he was out of your life," he said angrily. "Or was I just imagining that?"

"If you would stop for a second, I could explain that I fired Dallas today."

"You did?" Keith asked. That shut him up.

"Yes, I did. And he was here to discuss it. Okay?"

"Promise me you're not in love with him."

I looked him right in the eye and said, "I promise."

It felt wrong. But the alternative seemed more wrong. Sometimes the dice are just gonna come up snake eyes no matter how hard you blow.

Keith nodded but said nothing. I led him into the living room and he started banging out some chords on the piano.

I came up behind him and ran my hands down his chest while nuzzling him. "I'm sorry."

He turned and took my face in his hands.

"I'm sorry, too," he mumbled between kisses.

I led him over to the couch so that we might be more comfortable during the make-out session I was envisioning—that kind of sexy but angry kissing when you're not sure if you want to marry or murder the other person?

But when I pulled Keith on top of me, he backed off. Not off me, exactly, but away from me.

"I hate what this show is doing to us, Mallory. Do you ever think about . . . um . . . cutting back your workload?"

"You mean, like quit the show?"

"No, not quit, but like, maybe do a little less work? I mean, you work sixty hours a week on *Likely Story* and at least another twenty on schoolwork. I don't want to be just another thing you have to check off the list."

He had a point. Why was I doing all this work? Sixteen-year-olds do not need to be breadwinners. My mother, though no pillar of thrift, had lots of money tucked away in savings accounts and investments. We were not in danger of being sent to live in a paupers' prison. And my fantasies of going to an East Coast college with ivy-covered stone buildings were probably not being aided by my CliffsNotes-assisted analysis of Russian literature and my C-minus grasp of trig.

"I don't know, Keith. I do it because it's there."

Keith shrugged. "Maybe that's not such a good reason."

Maybe he was right. I refused to wallow, though. That was one thing my mother had taught me (even if she often forgot to follow her own advice). Instead, I got off the couch and changed the subject.

"How about some dinner?"

Our Hunter-Gatherer dinner was a staple of the latchkey kid diet: Paleozoic-era fish sticks I found at the back of the freezer next to the frozen woolly mammoth. I even whipped up a makeshift tartar sauce. (Thanks, Food Network!)

Keith and I had finished eating and were lounging at the kitchen table when my mother breezed into the room with a weary flair perfected over decades of attending charity events.

"Hello, princess," she said, as if she'd always called me this. "Did you get your homework done?"

She was in a strangely good mood. "There are some fish sticks left over if you're hungry," I offered.

"Oh, no, I'm on the liquid diet. They say I can lose twenty-five pounds in twenty-five days," she said brightly as she poured vodka into a health shake.

"You don't need to worry—you look great, ma'am," said Keith, working hard to ingratiate himself. He knew as well as I that this was a rare mood for her.

"Why, thank you, Keith," she cooed. Then she turned to me and said, "This one's a keeper, darling."

Okay. My mother was pleasant, remembered Keith's

name—heck, she even remembered I had homework. Had she switched her meds? It was either that or there was a new man in her life. I knew the patterns well.

Keith stood up. "I should probably get going," he said. "I have my own homework to blow off."

"I'll walk you out," I said.

When I got back to the house from delivering Keith to his car, I discovered my mother in the living room playing an old ABBA album. Yes, literally an album, on a turntable and everything. *Can you hear the drums, Fernando?*

I couldn't get one part of Keith's and my earlier conversation out of my head. Why was I working this hard? Maybe he was right. Maybe I should cut back. If the network was just going to undercut everything I was trying to do, what was the point of showing up? Let them have the show; I'd collect my royalties and fly to the Mexican Riviera for spring break.

I decided, against my better instincts, to engage my mother in conversation.

"You're in a chipper mood," I observed. "You haven't played ABBA since your last Emmy nom."

"I saw a commercial for *Mamma Mia!* today and I haven't been able to get 'Waterloo' out of my head. Besides, I'm excited for next week's premiere. Aren't you?"

I sighed. "I don't know. I guess. To be honest, it all seems to be spiraling out of control. Every time the network forces another change down my throat, I feel like I'm getting further and further away from the reason I even started this thing."

My mother slurped her spiked shake and asked, "What

was that reason again? Fame and fortune? Attention? Revenge against your mother?"

"I can barely remember. I mean, all those other things would be nice, but really I wanted to make a show that reflected the lives of real people. People I knew. But with that murder plotline it's like I can barely recognize my own show."

"Hmmm, that is a pickle, isn't it?" she said as she gulped down the last of the alcoholic slurry. "You know, one of the head writers of *Good As Gold* was in just such a predicament years ago. It was back in the eighties, when armed South American militants were all the rage. The network wanted my character to be kidnapped by a Colombian drug lord, but Manny Hiroshima was totally against it."

"What did he want to write about?" I asked.

"The ever-changing dynamics of couples in committed relationships. In other words—*boring*. But he wouldn't listen to anyone's advice. The network forced him to produce the Colombian storyline, but he secretly wrote a second script to his liking. We also filmed that. Then he showed the execs the scenes they wanted but edited in his scenes for broadcast. No one realized he'd switched the episodes until it was too late."

"Wow," I marveled. "That's courageous. What happened to him?"

"Oh, he was fired that day and never worked again."

"And the Colombian storyline?" I asked.

"They aired it the next day."

"So, was this supposed to be an inspirational anecdote?" I snapped.

My mother shrugged. "It was just a story. Take from it what you will." She paused, then asked, "What time is it?"

I glanced at my watch. "Eight-thirty," I said.

"Oh—time to take my diet pills."

I put my hand on her arm and said with genuine concern, "Mom, should you be taking those if you're doing the liquid diet thing? Isn't it dangerous to mix and match?"

My mother smiled. "You can never trust a doctor these days—with all the threats of malpractice swirling around, they're too afraid to give you the truly useful advice. You have to make it up on your own."

She toasted herself and laughed like she'd just landed a zinger on *Conan*. Then she ambled out of the room to the tune of imaginary applause.

I went back to my room, listened to the Smiths, and thought about dyeing my hair black. I kept trying to delve back into the Russian realism of *Anna Karenina* but was distracted by the NASCAR track my mind was racing around. I wanted to date Keith and be a normal girl. The constant bickering and drama was wearing me down. What was the point of all this work when the final product wasn't something I was going to be proud of?

I tossed Anna Karenina across the room, where she landed on the pile with David Copperfield, Mockingbird, and the other heroes of fiction that I had no time for. It was time to be the hero of my own life, even if it got me exiled from Hollywood.

I took a breath and started scribbling a whole new scenario on my yellow legal pad. Things were about to get dirty in this dry-clean-only town.

"I know all about your little escapade this afternoon," he said. "Your resourcefulness and leadership continue to impress me, but don't you think that this time they've led you straight off a cliff?"

twenty-five

Even though I'd told Richard I would never sacrifice the show for a relationship with anyone, I was convinced that this was the only way to *save* the show. Caution be damned, Dallas needed to stay. If I wanted anyone off, it was Alexis. I was not going to lose the one person I thought could make this show pop. Not if he wanted to stay.

I knew I was breaking one of my promises to Keith. It was going to take an intricate dance of rationalization and pleading for forgiveness for him to understand what I was doing. Hopefully, if I kept my other promises (being with him more, being with the show less, not being with Dallas at all), this one would be okay to break.

The plan was simple, if you call crazy and little hope for success "simple." It only involved duping the crew members, conspiring with the cast, blackmailing the editor, and "disappearing" Richard, my mother, and Frieda Weiner. ("Disappearing" is Hoffa-style Teamster slang for "getting rid of"—but we would be doing something a little less drastic than pouring them cement shoes for a walk off Santa Monica Pier.)

When I first arrived on set, I went straight to Dallas. If he wasn't on board, our ship was grounded. I knocked on his trailer door. He answered in his boxer shorts and nothing else. I tried not to look anywhere but his face.

"We need to talk," I said.

He ushered me inside and looked outside the door to make sure no one had seen us together. I didn't think this was necessary, but I liked that he sensed the covert nature of this operation from the get-go.

"What's up, Chief?" he asked.

"After our street-side conversation last night I wrote some new pages. I'm thinking we'd shoot these instead of your death by blade on Friday."

I slid the script pages across the table like they were top-secret government files. Dallas paged through them, scanning the contents.

"So I won't be killed off."

I nodded. "Are you in?"

He said nothing while he re-read parts. He looked up at me, and then back at the script. He tugged at his boxers nervously. I tried not to look.

"Based on real life much?" he asked.

"The world is my inspiration. Things like this happen—and it's a lot more real than teen murder rings."

Dallas took a deep breath and said, "I'm in. But will Richard let you do this?"

"No. That's why I'm not planning on telling him."

"You could be fired. We could both be fired."

"You were already fired," I pointed out. "But you don't have to agree. We could all get our futures handed to us in the form of pink slips. It's a risk. But I think it's our only chance to grab control of this show before it's too late."

He drummed his fingers on the table. "So what can I do to help?"

I leaned back in my chair and played with his iPod. "I need you to get Alexis on board."

"How am I supposed to do that?"

I shrugged. "Do you need me to paint you a picture?" I looked his body up and down. "What you're wearing will be fine."

With Dallas on board, my next stop was the makeup trailer. I knew that three other vital members of my black-ops team would be there: Javier, Francesca, and Gina.

Javier was gingerly holding a hot roller in his hair so that his curl would flip just so for that morning's scenes. Francesca was reading a book on Northern California camping.

"You camp?" I said, surprised.

"Totes," Francesca replied. "I was a Girl Scout. It's not all cookies, you know."

Gina entered the trailer. "What are all my Easter Peeps doing in here?" she said jovially.

I went to the door and locked it with the flimsy latch. I turned around and held my back against the door.

"What I'm about to propose may shock you, and any of you can opt out, no questions asked. But I need your help."

Javier immediately perked up, sitting forward like Lassie with his ears pointed forward. Francesca took a Bette Davis pose and reclined with an upraised eyebrow that murmured, *I'm intrigued.*

It was only Gina who clucked with a reserve of worry that surfaced in a disapproving, "I don't like the sound of this."

"Just hear me out. I'll take questions at the end. I think we can all agree on two things: One, this show is off-track like Sudan is off Broadway. Two, we need a change."

I took a breath and raised some script pages, dangling them like carrots.

"Someone who is scheduled to die on Friday isn't going to. It's simple, really, going back to what the show was supposed to be about. Francesca, you're going to leave Javier for Dallas. And he's going to leave Alexis for me. I mean, you. He's leaving Alexis for you."

"And how does Dallas feel about this?" Francesca asked, arching her other eyebrow.

"He's on board," I told her. "He wants to do this. Are you okay with that?"

"I have no problem if he has no problem," she said.

Gina finished pinning Javier's curl into place. I put my hand on her arm. "I need your help, too."

"What were you thinking, dear?"

"Have my mother take you out to lunch for your birthday. You've got to keep her off the set all afternoon. I can't trust her not to squeal if she figures out something's up."

"But it's not my birthday on Friday," Gina protested.

I rolled my eyes. "How long have you known my mother?"

"About three decades. Give or take."

"And has she ever remembered your birthday?"

Gina put down the eye shadow she was preparing for Francesca's face. "No, she never has."

"Then why would she start now? I'll even suggest it tonight. That way you don't have to bring it up."

Gina sighed her giving-in sigh. I'd heard it a million times before.

"I suppose. But I'm not going to tell anything other than white lies. No black ones."

I thanked her profusely. By now Javier was positively giddy with the excitement of the caper. "What can I do?" he asked eagerly.

"You, my friend, can help Greg break into the security office."

"What?" Greg nearly spilled his Vitaminwater when Javier and I found him in the commissary and told him what I needed him to do.

"I've been hanging around this studio since I was knee-high to a Munchkin," I explained. "So I know a few things. One is that Richie in security loves Chinese chicken salad. The other is that Groovy Gil the editor has been spending a whole lot of his work time using the network's equipment to edit his own hard-core horror movie."

"I don't see what Chinese chicken salad and Gil's horror movie have to do with anything," said Greg, straightening his skinny tie.

"This studio is totally Big Brother. There are security cameras *everywhere*."

Greg looked around for cameras, flop sweat beading on his forehead.

"If the bigwigs knew that Gil was spending so much of his time doing his own movie in the editing room, he might lose his job. I know that he pays off Richie. If you lure Richie out of the security office with the promise of CC salad, Javier can sneak in and abscond with the security tapes of Gil's extracurriculars. Then we can blackmail Gil into helping us cut the new scenes into the pilot without the network knowing."

"You're crazy," Greg said.

"Like a fox!" Javier whispered, clapping with glee.

"Will you do it?" I asked hopefully. "Please."

Greg looked me straight in the eye and said with all seriousness, "Just where are we going to get this Chinese chicken salad?"

"Chin Chin, silly," scolded Javier. "Best in LA."

My next stop on the super-secret express was Tamika. I was going to need her to use her film school skills to supervise Groovy Gil during his impromptu late-night editing session. Not surprisingly, she agreed right away to the covert operation and even vowed to wear all black that day just for fun. She was the only one who was sure this farce would work.

What I didn't expect was her cross-examination after she read the script I was planning to shoot. We were sitting outside on a memorial bench dedicated to some long-gone silent starlet who'd once walked these soundstage alleys.

Tamika cleared her throat. "Ahem, uh, this an *interesting* line you gave Dallas—'There's only one way out—through my bedroom.'"

"Yeah, what's wrong with that? I actually thought it was pretty good," I responded.

"This storyline is totally your fantasy fulfillment of Dallas whisking you away from Keith."

"It is not!" I protested.

Tamika just stared at me as if no response were necessary.

"Stop reading into it," I said. "You don't know what you're talking about. It's called *fiction*."

"Oh, come on. You think you're Alexis's character, huh? Sarah the innocent? Please! You are so totally Jacqueline, the misunderstood bad girl," Tamika said.

"Nuh-uh! I'm not a bad girl!" I exclaimed.

"I know you're not a 'bad girl.' That's why you're misunderstood. But try some reality—you writing about Ryan and Jacqueline in love is just an excuse to work out your Dallas issues. I mean, the way it is now, you want Ryan to end up with Jacqueline, not Sarah. That's quite a change."

"I don't have *Dallas issues*!"

"And I don't have weight issues," she said, not believing me. "Would you put your career on the line if it was anyone else on this set? Alexis? Never. Even for Javier or Francesca, you wouldn't."

"I would," I said, but the fight was knocked out of me. "If I thought it was for the good of the show . . . ," I went on, just trying to round out the rationalization. "Tamika. Be honest with me. Even if I do have feelings for Dallas—something I am *not* willing to admit at this time—are these pages any good? Am I kidding myself—or is this love triangle really the way to go? My gut is telling me it is, but I don't know if I can trust myself anymore."

Tamika stood up and looked into the hills behind the studio. She flicked her scarf and said matter-of-factly, "Darlin', these are the best damn scenes you've written yet. The story's a sizzler, and I'm not talkin' buffet."

Now we just had to make it all work.

"Officer! Arrest this girl!" Richard shouted. That's when I felt the cold, hard kiss of handcuffs on my wrists.

twenty-six

Like a good girl, I decided to ignore my feelings for Dallas and focus on fixing my relationship with Keith. I was hoping Keith would see that I couldn't just fire Dallas as some token of devotion. These were people's *lives* I was dealing with, and I didn't want to make professional decisions personal. I was pretty sure Keith would agree with me. He wasn't the kind of guy to hold a grudge. Or at least I didn't think he was. I'd never tested him like this.

I met him in the CPK parking lot, by his precious Ford Mustang. He'd restored it by hand, and I remembered how I'd wondered when we were first going out whether he'd ever love me as much as he loved his car. It was a beautiful car, much more beautiful than me, but I hoped that I gave more back. A few of our first dates had been in this car, just driving through the Hollywood Hills, laughing and talking and blasting the radio so all the neighborhoods could hear it. We bought Star Maps to see old celebrities' homes, and then made our own maps, these strange personal histories, and drove from crush's house to crush's house, ex's house to ex's house. It was the first time we drove past Erika's house that I found out she wasn't quite an ex, and that I was more than just a crush. It was a confusing time, but the way we rode together made me want to stay in the car and go forward.

He looked so tired, coming out the back door, leaving the kitchen behind. But then he saw me and he looked a shade more awake. It made me happy—relieved, really—that I could still do that to him.

We kissed hello.

"What's up?" he asked.

"What are you doing Friday afternoon?" I asked demurely.

"You tell me," he said with a smirk.

"I need you to ditch school."

"Done and done. What for?"

I paused. Did I really want to involve him in this? No, not really. But I couldn't figure out how to do it without him. I wanted him to be my partner (in crime). I jumped right in and told him my plan to hijack production on Friday and film new scenes for the pilot. He nodded seriously, asked a few questions about logistics, but was generally supportive.

"You're taking this really well," I said, mildly surprised.

"Why wouldn't I?" he asked.

"Because . . . I don't know if you've realized this . . . but if I manage to pull this off, it means that Dallas won't be leaving the show. At least not for the foreseeable future."

Keith nodded his Zen Buddhist nod again. I couldn't tell what he was thinking.

"So . . . ?" I prompted.

"This is important to you, right?"

I nodded.

"Then it's important to me, too."

I loved him so much right then.

"Thank you, Keith," I said, hugging him tightly. "Thank you for understanding. I was afraid you might go totally berserk on me for not firing Dallas. I thought you'd be jealous or . . . worse."

He stroked my hair and intertwined his leg with mine. "I've kinda been thinking about things, you know? Sure, I'm jealous of Dallas. He's a good-looking guy who spends all day with my girlfriend. But, like, we're gonna have to deal with stuff like that if we're gonna last, am I right?"

"How did I get so lucky?" I asked.

"My mom also said breaking up with you would be the stupidest thing I'd done since I broke my arm skateboarding down the up escalator at the Westside Pavilion in the seventh grade. There's one thing I don't understand, though, Mallory," he said.

"What's that?"

"I don't have any film skills like Tamika and I'm not on your show. What do you need me to do Friday afternoon?"

"How do you feel about being the world's worst chauffeur?"

Richard and I were scheduled to attend a press junket on Friday morning. Basically, we'd talk to various local news outlets and cable networks, selling the show like we were QVC hosts. New and Improved! Tastes Better! Less Fat!

It took place at the Beverly Hilton, former home of Trader Vic's and perpetual home of Hollywood's dumbest awards, the Golden Globes. Tons of reporters from *Access Hollywood* to KIIS-FM were there. We'd had to arrive at 6 a.m. and were immediately busy answering the same questions for sixty-five different reporters.

My mind was hardly on the interviews. All I could think about was whether my scheme was going to work. I tried to smile and let Richard do the talking, but naturally, my very teen-ness was half the story, so the interviewers lobbed a lot of questions my way. *Yes, it was fun growing up the daughter of a soap star. No, I think I'm just as normal as everyone else. Yes, it is hard balancing work and school, but I'm managing.* These were all lies, of course, but you don't want John Q. Public to know the truth. And even if he does know, he doesn't want to hear you talk about it.

After we were done, Richard and I walked down to the hotel lobby to wait for our car. It was also the second step of my plan. The first had been to stuff a few sleeping pills into his last Diet Coke with lemon.

"Shall we stop somewhere and grab a power lunch? I think we deserve it after the press gauntlet," Richard said. "Then we can go enjoy watching Dallas get murdered."

Not on your life, I thought, but I said, "Oh, gee, thanks. I can't, though. I have to stop by my school to drop off some work."

This wasn't entirely untrue, since I was supposed to drop off my paper on *Anna Karenina*. The slight problem there was that I hadn't actually written the paper, so there was little point in going to school. I was sure the school would understand if it was late—just like every other time. The main thing was that I had to separate from Richard.

"I'll just meet you back at the studio," I finished.

"We took the same limo here, Mallory."

I was ready for this. "That's okay—you take the limo. My friend is picking me up. She'll drop me off."

The truth of the matter was, I would, in fact, be taking the limo back to the studio. But Richard would be taking the other limo I'd rented (and that Keith was driving) on a six-hour joyride around Los Angeles County's outer ring. And there it was, Richard's special limo, pulling off Santa Monica Boulevard and into the parking lot.

"That's you," I said.

Keith pulled up and parked. He got out of the car and went around to open the door. I was gambling that Richard was too self-absorbed to notice that Keith was not the original driver and that this was not the original limo. My gamble paid off. Richard got in without so much as acknowledging Keith.

Once he shut the door, Keith turned to me, winked, and said, "Let's go to Big Bear this weekend, Sundance."

He'd finally invited me to Big Bear. That meant a camping weekend—a big step. This relationship *was* going places.

"Sounds great, Butch," I said.

"Did you slip him the pills?" he asked.

"Enough to put him to sleep, but not enough for you to have to take him to the ER. He should be fast asleep in about fifteen minutes."

"See you at the rendezvous," Keith said.

He tipped his hat and was on his way.

It was time to get to work.

Gina and my mother were out to lunch at The Grill as planned. I knew it would be impossible for my mother to resist a spin through Neiman Marcus once she was that close, so I was confident they wouldn't be back on set until at least sundown. That gave me about five hours to film the six scenes I had written, set to air in two days.

I had decided the only way to deal with the crew was to be a bulldog. I figured that if I barked loud enough, everyone else would just whimper.

I walked onto Stage 4 and found the director, Kadir. We had a brief tête-à-tête about how we would now be filming new pages that were "hot off the presses." I handed him my "revised" script and he stared at it in disbelief.

"These aren't even the same setups," he complained.

"Sets and camera angles can't dictate creative inspiration," I said wearily, as if his problems were the last thing I needed to hear. Of course, he was rightly upset that he'd planned for one thing and now I was changing it to another, but I just tried to act like Richard in response. He would expect people to change course, at any given moment, according to his whims.

"Well, what does Richard say?" Kadir asked.

"He's taken the rest of the day off. He was really tired after the press junket this morning. He left everything in my hands."

Kadir took this pretty casually. Senior execs taking Fridays off was hardly a shocker. He scanned the pages again and said sullenly, "Yeah, we should be able to get most of this done. And you know what? I like this much better. I'm glad you're not killing off Ryan."

I told him that he had to get it all done, no matter what. If we didn't get this done today, I'd never have another chance and *Likely Story* would go on the air in its bastardized version, and that was not going to happen on my watch. I didn't tell him this. I just told him these scenes had better be in the can by the end of the day or we were all in trouble.

My phone vibrated in my pocket. I took it out and read Greg's text message:

GOT THE TAPE. C U AT EDIT BAY.

Nice. Javier and Greg had pulled off Operation Chinese Chicken Salad. It was possible that the editor would go along just like Kadir had gone along—but if he didn't, we now had a little blackmail. There was only one more hurdle: a little princess named Alexis. Dallas was supposed to have buttered her up (not literally), but I had held off giving her the script lest she go crying to Richard and ruin my plan.

When Alexis walked on the set in tears, I knew Dallas had finally given her the new scenes.

"Honey, what's wrong?" I said, as if I was just at wits' end trying to please her.

"You're changing the whole story! With Ryan dead, I was going to be the star! And if Ryan's not dead, I want him to be in love with Sarah!" she heaved.

"It's just a minor change," I lied. "It's just to add a bit of drama."

"Don't you think I'm a good actress?" she went on, inconsolable.

"Of course I do. Everyone does. But since you're so upset, we should shoot the scene where you find out that he's leaving you. We should do it right now so you can use this."

Alexis nodded. "I can definitely use this. Let's go."

From that moment on, we didn't let up. As a result, the shoot went pretty quickly. It was amazing how good the crew was at churning this stuff out. They even applauded after a couple of particularly juicy takes. We weren't going to have much time to edit these together, so I was taking copious notes about which shots I wanted to use.

Dallas was striking in most every scene, especially when he delivered the line "There's only one way out—through my bedroom." Francesca fell into his arms and I knew from the second they locked lips that this was a romance I wanted to watch. The chemistry had never really popped between Dallas and Alexis, and now even though Sarah was going to try to get Ryan back, it wasn't going to be a fair fight.

Meanwhile, Javier and Alexis were dynamite, like Posh and Becks, only American. When she crumpled into tears, spurned by her boyfriend, it was both pitiable and electric. And then the final scene in the forest, when Marco confronted Ryan about stealing Jacqueline, was positively explosive. Dallas and Javier were both experts at stage fighting and pulled off several impressive moves.

I told the PA in charge of the tapes to drop them at the edit bay right away. Then I raced upstairs to find Greg.

Only there was someone standing in my way.

Frieda Weiner.

"I know what you're up to," she said sweetly. "Don't think you're going to get away with it. I saw you on the monitors!"

My first impulse was to push her into a closet and lock it. But here's where the real world differs from the soap opera world: In the real world, there's no such thing as a closet that locks from the outside.

I tried to figure out what Richard would do in this situation, but I came up with a total blank. Then I realized I had a deeper source of power.

What would my mother do? I thought.

And that gave me my answer.

I smiled back just as sweetly and fakely at Frieda Weiner as she was smiling at me.

"I don't care what you think, you small, pathetic *consultant*," I purred condescendingly. "This is not your show. It has never been your show, and it never will be your show. If the network wanted you to run a show, they would have hired you to run a show, not to *consult*. While I *appreciate* your opinion, the time for indulging it is long past. I'm tired of you, Frieda Weiner. Now get out of my way, so I can do my job."

Frieda Weiner's smile slipped, like I'd knocked it right from her face.

"Why, I'll tell Trip Carver!" she gasped.

"You've already tried to tell Trip Carver," I said calmly. "And your calls didn't even make it through."

This was total guesswork on my part, but the confirmation was clear on the catty consultant's dumbstruck face.

Thank you, Greg, I thought. *You were right not to put her calls through.*

I put my hand on her shoulder consolingly. All I touched was shoulder pad.

"Look," I said, "I can't fire you, but I can definitely make your whole life miserable. Go home. Take a bubble bath. Look for a new job. Go ruin someone else's show. You're not going to ruin mine."

And with that, I simply walked away.

An exit, my mother always said, was as important as any entrance. Usually better because you were nearly *guaranteed* applause.

The editing bays were in their own little cavern in the basement of the production office building. Fortunately, by this time on a Friday, most of the office staff had gone home. It was empty except for Tamika, who sat near reception reading *American Cinematographer*. She stood up as soon as I arrived.

"Are we a go?" she asked.

I held up the tape as a response.

"I watched the feed today—the dailies look great," she said supportively.

"Stay out here and wait for the videotapes to arrive from the set. Don't let anyone back there," I told her.

"Aye, aye, Cap'n," she said with a salute and a click of her heels.

I slunk down the corridor, hoping to avoid any stragglers coming out of the copy room.

I made it to the edit suite and found Gil hard at work on his own movie.

"Evening, Gil," I said cheerily.

"Hi there, Mallory, how's it hangin'?" he drawled, trying to block the screen.

"Hard at work on company time?" I asked. This was too easy; I wouldn't even need the blackmail.

"Yeah, and then I'm driving up to Monterey tonight to go camping with some pals from Burning Man."

"That sounds like fun. But you should plan on getting a late start," I said.

"Huh?"

"I'm sorry to do this, Gil, I really am. But I think you're going to have to work overtime tonight."

Much to my surprise, Gil took the whole thing in stride. If anything, he was impressed with my resourcefulness. He even made a couple of comments saying how much he was groovin' on the new scenes.

We had just finished splicing in the last scene and Tamika was already packing up her bag when my phone rang. It was a restricted number. Usually I don't answer unlisted calls. But something told me I had better pick it up.

"Hello?" I said with forced breeziness. But the breeze completely stopped when I heard who was calling.

"What is it?" Tamika asked with alarm when I hung up.

I gulped. I couldn't believe this was really happening.

"Keith's in jail," I said. "Richard had him arrested for attempted kidnapping."

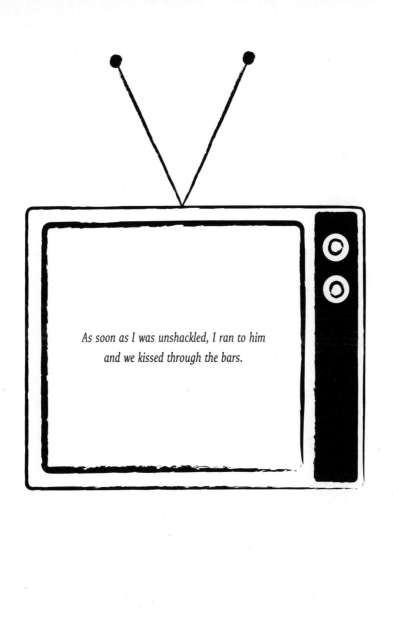

As soon as I was unshackled, I ran to him and we kissed through the bars.

twenty-seven

It took Tamika and me over an hour and a half to get to the Rancho Cucamonga police station in Friday traffic.

I had never been in a real police station before, only the set that had passed for both the police station and the post office in *Good As Gold*. Nothing quite prepares you for the dank stench of the law. I went to the officer sitting behind a sign that read *Inquiries* and asked for Keith.

The desk sergeant looked up at me and said, "You mean the kidnapper?"

"He's *not* a kidnapper!" I pleaded. "I need to see him. He's my boyfriend."

"Oh, well, then. I didn't realize he was your *boyfriend*. In that case, he *still* won't be available until he's arraigned Monday morning."

"Monday morning?!" I was flabbergasted. "Don't you see? This has all been a terrible, terrible mistake. Is it bail money you want? Because I have credit cards and I'm not afraid to use them."

"I wondered how long it would take for you to show your scheming face," a voice said from behind me.

"Excuse me," I said to the officer before turning around to face Richard.

He was sitting in a plastic bucket seat with a tattered issue of *Inland Empire Living* in his lap. His eyes looked a bit heavy.

"Keith has nothing to do with this," I told him. "Drop the charges, or whatever you have to do."

"Ha!" he cackled. "Hi, Tamika, nice of you to turn this wanted woman in. I see a promotion in your future."

"What are you talking about, Richard?" I fumed.

He held up a can of Diet Coke with one hand. Then he held out a few semi-dissolved sleeping pills in the other.

"I'd recognize your mother's generic Mexican pills any-where. And any fool knows that it takes *exactly* twenty-six minutes for them to dissolve in soda."

I started to back away, unsure of what he was threatening.

"I know you tried to drug me, Mallory. And if you bothered to watch *Law and Order,* you'd know that makes you part of the conspiracy to commit kidnapping. A felony in this state."

Tamika gasped. I looked over to her and then back at Richard and said, "You're insane if you think that'll stick."

"That's not my problem. It's yours. Officer! Arrest this girl!" Richard shouted.

That's when I felt the cold, hard kiss of handcuffs on my wrists.

The next thirty minutes were possibly the longest thirty min-utes I have ever spent staring at a cinder block wall painted yellow. Occasionally, through the little Plexiglas window of my holding cell, I would see another person being led through the halls. They all seemed drunk.

Then, suddenly, a female officer whose tag read *Joan* opened the cell door.

"You're gettin' moved," she said sternly. This was not a pleasant woman. I suppose I couldn't blame her. There was no way for her to realize this was all a big misunderstanding and we really hadn't meant any harm. All we were trying to do was sabotage a major network television program, not kill or kidnap anyone. Surely she'd see the humor in that.

Joan led me through a couple of other hallways via doors that locked on both sides. We spent more time waiting for her to find the right key than we did walking. Finally, we ended up outside a more traditional kind of cell, the kind with bars that you can rattle a can on. She threw me into one of two cells. Keith was in the other.

"Keith!" I exclaimed upon seeing him.

"Mallory!" he said, shocked to see me in handcuffs. As soon as I was unshackled, I ran to him and we kissed through the bars.

"No kissing!" Joan hollered.

We separated immediately like frightened alley cats.

He held up his hand and said, "To revolution."

"And anarchy . . . ," I said feebly.

"Why were you arrested?" he asked.

"I'm so sorry—it's all my fault," I sobbed.

Joan hollered again, "No talking!"

We sat in silence for the next ten minutes, staring at each

other from our matching benches. We spent the time watching the sliver of sunlight crawl across the floor. All I could think about was how much trouble I'd gotten Keith into.

You went to jail for me, I thought. *Now I can never dump you. Ever.*

Mercifully, Joan walked out through a door, telling us she'd be right back. We decided to risk talking.

"I'm so sorry," I said.

"It was his cell phone," he told me. "We forgot about his cell phone. He was sleeping for some of the time. And other times I tried to drive places where there wasn't any reception. But after a while, he figured out something was wrong, and that I wasn't just lost. He started to yell at me—I don't know how you can stand it—and then finally he called the cops and we were pulled over. I didn't know what to say. I told him you were playing a prank—I didn't tell him about the show, I promise."

"Oh, Keith, that doesn't matter," I said. "What matters is that we get out of here. Have I happened to mention how sorry I am?"

He smiled. "Don't be. It was fun—well, until the cops showed up."

The door opened, and Joan returned . . . this time with Richard.

"I'd like to speak with them alone if you don't mind," he said to Joan.

Strangely, she agreed and left the three of us alone. I thought that was one of those things that only happened in soap operas, like the time my mother confronted the man who'd tried to strangle her with a necktie and got him to confess to being her supposedly dead evil ex-husband with a new face (and body) mysteriously ten years younger. Only this time was going to be different. I wasn't going to confess to anything.

"We're not saying anything to you or anyone else until we have a chance to speak to a lawyer," I told him bluntly.

Richard just smiled. "It's all right, princess. I can do the talking for a while. You see, Tamika already appealed to my sense of mercy and told me everything. Now that I have phone service again, I was able to check in with some of our friends—Kadir, Gil, Trip. I also had the most *illuminating* voice mails from Alexis and Frieda Weiner."

He paused to study my reaction. I tried to stay calm, but I'm sure my real feelings were peeking through.

Richard walked over to the bars, put one hand on them, and leaned in.

"I know all about your little escapade this afternoon," he said. "Your resourcefulness and leadership continue to impress me, but don't you think that this time they've led you straight off a cliff?"

I sighed and turned away. "I had no choice, Richard."

"You have nothing but choices, Mallory. And I'm about to give you one more. You give me total control of the show from here on out and I, in turn, will drop the charges against you and your misguided boyfriend."

"Wh-what?" I stammered. I was still in shock from the events of the previous few hours.

"You heard me. I want the keys to Deception Pass, and in exchange I will give you two your freedom. It's really a very good deal."

"Don't do it, Mallory. We can get lawyers," Keith said.

It was true. We could afford lawyers. Good lawyers, even. But what was the point? Richard had beaten me at my own game. I was outmaneuvered and backed into a corner. I might have choices, but none of them were good. There was one thing I could save right now: Keith's reputation. Mine was gone. He certainly didn't need an arrest for kidnapping on his application to Stanford.

I looked at the challenge in Richard's eyes. He was waiting for my answer.

And I realized what it had to be.

I had to give him the answer he wanted.

"No," I said.

He grinned and raised an eyebrow.

"No?" he asked.

"No," I said. "I love this show. As you can see, I will do anything for this show. You already have one set of keys to Deception Pass. But I'm keeping my set."

"Really?" Richard challenged.

"Really," I said from behind bars. "Plus, the last thing you want is for me to be arrested. There isn't a paper or blog in America that won't carry the story. And although I know you think there's no such thing as bad publicity, deep down you know there is. Yeah, a scandal will get people to tune in—but only for a week. You want this show to last for years. And if you and I get into a tabloid fight, you know that I will play the little innocent princess card and you will become the big bad producer. I'm a young, somewhat attractive daughter of a much-loved soap star. You're a suit. Who do you think they'll side with, Richard? What makes a better story?"

"Mallory, wait!" Keith tried to interrupt.

"No, no," Richard said. "I'm enjoying this. Although you'd have such better footing on your higher ground if you hadn't tried to kidnap and kill me."

"I wasn't trying to kill you!"

"You have your spin, I have mine." Richard turned away from the bars, opened the door, and ushered Joan the police officer back into the room.

Her hand was on her pistol.

"I want one thing clear," Richard said to me. "While I certainly underestimated you, you also underestimated me. *Massively* underestimated me. Yes, I was tired of Dallas's tantrums and was ready to kill his character off. But if you changed your mind, you should have told me. We all have our secrets, Mallory—lord knows I'm keeping one or two myself—but there comes a time to share them. That's judgment, Mallory. And while you've shown some excellent skills today, judgment isn't particularly one of them.

"So I talked to Kadir and Gil, and, under a bit of duress, Trip's assistant managed to e-mail me some of the footage. You know what, Mallory? Everyone's in agreement. It's great television. Absolutely great television. Whatever you did on the set today, you did right. Dallas and the others have never been so good. Finally, they're feeling it."

Even behind bars, this was a huge relief to me.

Richard looked at me and Keith. "So, Bonnie and Clyde, did you ever watch my show *Three-Alarm Fire?*"

"No," I said flatly.

"Yeah!" Keith exclaimed.

"Now, doesn't Joan here look a little familiar to you?"

Keith stared at her, then smiled for the first time all night.

"She was the cop who'd always show up at the scene," he said.

Richard nodded. "Yes, Joan was one of our advisors, and every now and then, we'd have a part for her. Just like today."

It took a moment for me to process this.

"So she's not really a cop?"

Richard laughed. "No, she's very much a cop. And this is very much a police station. And you're very much arrested."

All my hopes deflated.

"But," Richard continued, "I bet with a good word from me, it'll be like this never happened."

Joan moved her hand away from her pistol and nodded.

"I pledge to stop underestimating you if you promise to stop underestimating me," Richard said, offering his hand through the bars.

I shook it.

"You have yourself a deal," I said.

"The poison apple doesn't fall far
from the tree," she said.

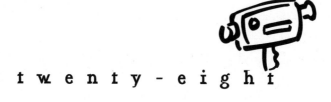

twenty-eight

My mother was waiting for me the moment I walked in the door.

"That was quite a stunt you pulled," she said. "Richard told me everything!"

"It's late," I said. "I'm tired."

"My own daughter, a felon!"

"I'm not a felon."

"You're lucky Richard is so darling. I would have let you stay there for a week."

"Thanks, Mother."

She was wearing one of those nightgowns that could double as a ball gown, as if a gentleman caller might stop in at any moment. But instead of Tom, Brick, or Harry, all she had was me.

"You're very lucky it was Gina's birthday today," she went on. "Otherwise, I might have smelled out your unholy machinations!"

"Mom. Please." I really needed sleep. Richard and I were going to spend the whole weekend polishing the show.

"Did you think *for one moment* about what it would have meant to my reputation if you'd been caught? Did you think *for one small second* about how your script changes affect *my* role?"

"No," I told her honestly. "You didn't cross my mind at all."

She nodded and looked satisfied, although I wasn't sure what exact point she'd just proven to herself.

"The poison apple doesn't fall far from the tree," she said. And then she surprised me by adding, "You're *just like* your father."

This was her exit line, and she made the most of it.

My father. My unknown father.

She'd definitely managed to leave me speechless.

We watched the first episode so many times that weekend that I stopped being able to see it with any kind of objectivity. Did it suck? Was it great? I couldn't tell. Richard called in the cast and crew so we could tweak the rest of the week's episodes in line with the premiere. Mostly, this involved Francesca and Dallas, who were both willing to do anything we asked.

"This is really working," Francesca admitted to me between takes on Saturday. "We've finally hit the mark."

Dallas, Francesca, Alexis, and Javier were all flying out to New York on Sunday night so they could do the morning shows on Monday.

When the taping was done, Dallas gave me a hug goodbye. And I had to wonder if he'd hugged me only because Javier had hugged me right before him. But something told me it meant a little bit more. Or was that just wishful thinking?

I holed myself up in the editing room with Richard and Gil, then needed a break and went down to the set. Nobody else was around—it was just me and Deception Pass.

For a moment—just a single moment—I allowed myself to think it:

All of this exists because of me.

Everything I was seeing, everything I was walking through, had started off in my head. The guidance office. The picnic area. Ryan's house. Sarah's bedroom.

"It feels good, doesn't it?" a voice asked.

I turned around, and there was Dallas, stepping out of the shadows.

"Aren't you supposed to be on a plane?" I asked.

"The car's picking me up here," he answered. "I just wanted to stop by one more time, to see it all before it becomes real."

"You just wanted one more walk on the set?"

"And I wanted to see you. To wish you luck."

"Wish *us* luck," I said.

"That, too."

We were standing in the middle of the set, midway between Jacqueline's kitchen and the garage where Ryan worked.

"Mallory . . . ," he said, leaning closer in the shadows.

"What?" I asked.

"Thank you."

Someone should have yelled, "CUT!" The cameras should have stopped. The next scene should have been called.

But this wasn't a show. This was two people and their closeness. This was so many things unspoken, and a few things said.

He was so beautiful at that moment.

And in his eyes, I was beautiful, too.

"Thank you for saving me from myself," he whispered.

"Right now you're going to have to save me from myself," I whispered back.

There was a flicker of a second when he moved in to kiss me. But then he understood. And he pulled back.

"I'm sorry," he said.

"Don't be. Please."

He shook his head. "I still can't believe you and Keith went to jail!"

Once the name was out in the open, there was no way we could do anything. We both knew that.

"It was pretty crazy," I said, conversational now. "And look at you—about to return to New York and brave the morning talk show hosts. That's scarier than jail."

"My friends from Juilliard are planning to picket outside the *Good Morning America* windows," he said with a smile. "I say, let 'em have their Shakespeare. I'm happy here."

Now it was my turn to say, "Thank you."

He wrapped me in a hug, this one closer than the one before.

I could feel the cab waiting for him in the distance. I could feel Keith waiting for me to call. I could feel Richard needing me in the editing room for one last look.

So I let Dallas go, pretending I had no choice.

The opening credits began to roll on Likely Story. *I held my breath.*

twenty-nine

Because most of the cast was off in New York, we didn't tape on Monday. Instead, I stayed at home and stressed out about the premiere.

At around noon, the phone rang. Since my mother was at a spa treatment, I picked up.

"Hello?" I said.

"To whom am I speaking?" a crinkly voice asked.

"Mallory. Who is this?"

"Aren't you on the set of your television show?"

I couldn't place the voice, but it sounded vaguely familiar. "No," I said. "We have the day off. Who is this?"

"Are you with your tutor?"

Miss Julie? It hadn't even crossed my mind.

"Who is this?" I repeated. And then I realized who it was: My school secretary.

"Young lady, may I speak to your mother?"

"She's not home."

"Well, have her call me *immediately*. If you're not at work, you should be in school!"

I had a feeling this spelled trouble. But I put it out of my mind as three o'clock rolled around.

Greg was the first to arrive, with an armful of flowers.

"From Trip," he said. "But I wrote the card."

I opened it and found:

> To my amazing, risk-taking friend.
> Here's to a long, long Story.
> love, Greg

"Take off your tie and stay awhile," I told him. And he did.

My mother made the next entrance.

"I'm watching in my room," she announced. Then she glided off, without even wishing me luck.

Keith and Scooter came as soon as school ended, with Gina and Tamika arriving a minute later.

"It's a party!" Scooter proclaimed. And I thought, yes, it *was* a party. For my mother, a party might mean a lavishly catered affair with musicians and speeches and champagne. But this was the kind of party I loved—a group of friends in the living room, with bags of cookies and chips and Hawaiian Punch, ready to watch a show we'd all had a part in, whether big or small.

Perversely, I wished for a second that Amelia could have joined us, or even that I could have invited her. But that seemed like ancient history now.

"I'm really excited," Keith said with encouragement as he settled in on the couch. "You haven't shown me jack from this show, so I'm dying to see it."

"Don't get your hopes up," I said. Then, sitting next to

him, I added, "I just want you to know that no matter what you think of this show, I love you."

"I love you, too," he said as he fiddled with the buttons to achieve optimal surround sound on the plasma TV.

I grabbed his arm. "No, I'm serious. I really love you and no one in this world except for you would have put himself on the line for me like you did. I am forever in your debt."

Keith rolled his eyes and gave me a popcorn-flavored kiss. "Shut up—I know the difference between TV and real life. I can only hope I see myself in there."

That's when the opening credits began to roll on *Likely Story*.

I held my breath. Scooter, Tamika, and Greg cheered.

The theme music played. It sounded like a torch song you'd sing late at night and downstairs in a New York City jazz club. First, there was the shot of the fog-shrouded two-pronged bridge. There were the pine trees glowing like candles in the setting sun. That was followed by most of the shots I'd gotten on our shoot in Deception Pass. Alexis glowed. Javier sulked. Francesca exuded mystery. And Dallas looked hot. Mission: Impossible accomplished.

The first scene was Friday afternoon's scene with Dallas and Alexis.

RYAN walks into SARAH'S
BEDROOM and closes the door
like a spy seeking plutonium.

RYAN
I'm leaving.

>   SARAH
>   But you just got here.
>
>   RYAN
>   I'm leaving *you*.
>
>   SARAH
>   But, Ryan! You can't! You
>   just *can't*!
>
>   RYAN
>   I'm sorry. I'm in love with
>   someone else. And her name is
>   Jacqueline.

"Take that, Alexis," I said.

"Shhh. I'm watching," Keith said, staring intently at the box.

Keith held my hand through the first ten minutes. It cut to commercial and everyone told me it was great. I felt good, because I felt like I was telling the story I wanted to tell.

My mother's scenes in the counseling office were just as ridiculous as they'd seemed on the set. But somehow, the sheer act of their being transmitted over the airwaves made them camp. Instead of being stupid, they were *entertaining*. Keith was laughing all the way through them.

"Hysterical!" he said.

I wondered if my mother knew this. I hadn't known. But I bet she had. My mother knew a lot of things I didn't give her credit for.

As the hour was wrapping up, we came to the climactic scene, when Jacqueline is confronted by her boyfriend, Marco, and her new love, Ryan.

>   MARCO bangs at the door of
>   RYAN'S CONDO. JACQUELINE
>   turns to RYAN.
>
>
>   JACQUELINE
>   I knew he'd find us here.
>
>
>   RYAN
>   There's only one way out—
>   through my
>   bedroom.
>
>
>   JACQUELINE looks RYAN in the
>   eye. She knows it might not
>   be a proposal, but it's the
>   best she can expect. She
>   kisses him just as MARCO
>   storms in.
>
>
>   RYAN
>   Too late.
>
>
>   And BLACKOUT.

Keith howled with approval. "Yowza! That's some hot tamales you just served up. I'm so proud of you!"

I couldn't believe he liked it. I couldn't believe it had aired just like I had imagined. I couldn't believe he'd either missed or ignored the parallels to our own lives. I couldn't believe the world hadn't stopped turning. I had a show on the air and everything kept moving.

I looked at my silenced phone. Immediately the messages began to rack up. Congratulations from Trip, from Richard. And from Dallas, a single "bravo."

"You did it," Greg said.

And I thought, yes, I had done it.

With a little help from my friends.

My mother waited until everyone had left before emerging from her bedroom. It was almost six o'clock, and she was dressed for a night out.

"Well?" I asked from my perch on the couch. I was re-watching the episode, this time with my laptop at the ready for any notes I wanted to take.

"They did a wonderful job with the lighting," she replied.

I couldn't believe it.

"They air the first episode of my show and all I can get out of you is a 'They did a wonderful job with the lighting'?"

"Surely I didn't teach you to be so touchy," she said. "The show was good. Very good, even. But don't rest on your laurels. You must always try to make it better. If I coddled you with my praise, you'd never grow up. Of course, I feel pride toward you. But you can't expect me to constantly express it, in the same way that I don't expect you to constantly express your pleasure with my performance."

"You were great, Mom," I said, knowing it meant nothing now that she'd fished for it.

"Thank you. I was pleased with it myself." She looked at her watch. "Oh, I'm late for my date. Get some sleep tonight. You'll need it."

"Why?"

She looked at me like I'd just asked her how to turn on the television.

"*Why?* Because the biggest test of all comes in the morning."

"And that would be?"

"The ratings, darling," she said. "Tomorrow morning, we shall all live or die by the ratings."

I was about to tell her that she didn't need to scream when it occurred to me that she wasn't screaming to me. There was someone else in the house.

thirty

There were about twenty seconds after I woke up when I forgot about the verdict that was about to come. Instead, I woke up looking forward to the day. I was looking forward to Dallas and Francesca and Javier being back in town. I was looking forward to seeing Keith after work and planning our trip to Big Bear. I was looking forward to going to the writers' office with Tamika and the rest of them so we could write more and more and more of *Likely Story*. I was looking forward to dragging Greg away from Trip's phone for an hour so he could eat lunch.

And then I remembered the ratings.

I leaped for my laptop, hoping someone had e-mailed them to me. But my laptop wasn't there—I'd left it in the living room. My hair in knots, my pajamas looking as unflattering as pajamas can, I headed downstairs. As I made my way through the foyer and past the solarium, I heard something buzzing in the library. Of course—my mother's antique fax machine. Though she seemed to enjoy the Internet, she never quite took to e-mail. She still insisted that everything be sent to her

293

via fax. "I like paper; it feels good between my fingers," she'd once said.

Unspooling from the mahogany desk were the Overnights, a.k.a. the Nielsen ratings for yesterday's episode. Were they good? Were they abysmal? I was afraid to look. But I had to. I had to know. I grabbed the paper from the tray. But all I saw was a parade of numbers that made no sense to me. It might as well have been an AP Calculus test. I had no hope of deciphering them.

"Well, well, well," my mother said from the hallway. She was wearing her fancy nightgown, the one with gemstones and pearls embroidered into the silky gauze. "Are those the ratings?" she asked.

"Looks like it."

"How are they?"

"I don't know."

She grabbed the paper from me like a rabid coyote devouring a toy poodle. She scanned them quickly. I tried to read her face. Good? Bad? Middling?

"Oh my God!" she cried. "They're SPECTACULAR!!!" She took another look and screamed, "Darling, the ratings are through the roof!"

I was about to tell her that she didn't need to scream when it occurred to me that she wasn't screaming to me. There was someone else in the house.

Richard appeared in the doorway. He was wearing an oversized burgundy terry-cloth robe with my mother's initials monogrammed on the lapel. I grabbed for the desk to steady myself.

"They're good, are they?" he asked my mother while he

sipped a mimosa. Then he saw me. "Ah, Mallory. I didn't expect to see you so soon. It sounds like our show's a hit." He
air-toasted me.

"What are you d-doing here?" I stammered.

"We're celebrating, can't you tell?" my mother interjected
cheerily, lifting her own mimosa.

"Mallory," Richard said, his smile uncontrollable, "it's
about time you knew. Your mother and I are very much in
love. And we're going to get married."

What else could I do?

I sputtered out a congratulations.

Then I fell to the floor, and the world went black.

About the Author(s)

David Van Etten splits himself between three minds and three bodies. They belong to:

David Levithan can't remember who he is. He was found wandering the streets of Manhattan, clutching a red scarf. In his backpack were many books that look to be written by him. He cannot remember writing them. Every time he sees a photo of a UFO, he shivers.

David Ozanich was fortunate to escape the clutches of a South American drug cartel in time to attend the London premiere of his play *The Lightning Field*. When not traveling the world as an internationally acclaimed playwright, he enjoys kidnapping, backstabbing, and scheming.

Before becoming a writer for ABC's *One Life to Live,* **Chris Van Etten** was a private eye. Before that, he was a professional gambler, and before that: a stable boy. He is currently considering a career as police commissioner.

To read more about David Van Etten, be sure to check out www.myspace.com/davidvanetten.

David Van Etten's next book about Mallory, *Red Carpet Riot,* will be available Summer 2009.